Women and Ghosts

BY ALISON LURIE

Fiction

Love and Friendship
The Nowhere City
Imaginary Friends
Real People
The War Between the Tates
Only Children
Foreign Affairs
The Truth About Lorin Jones
The Oxford Book of Modern Fairy Tales (editor)
Women and Ghosts

Nonfiction

The Language of Clothes
Don't Tell the Grown-Ups

For Children

The Heavenly Zoo
Clever Gretchen and Other Forgotten Folktales
Fabulous Beasts

ALISON LURIE

Women and Ghosts

NAN A. TALESE

DOUBLEDAY

New York London Toronto Sydney Auckland

PUBLISHED BY NAN A. TALESE
an imprint of Doubleday
a division of
Bantam Doubleday Dell Publishing Group, Inc.
1540 Broadway, New York, New York 10036

DOUBLEDAY is a trademark of Doubleday, a division of
Bantam Doubleday Dell Publishing Group, Inc.

The following stories have been published, in slightly different form,
as follows: "Fat People" and "The Pool People" in *Vogue;* "Ilse's House"
in *New York Woman;* "The Highboy" in *Redbook;* and "Counting
Sheep" in *Southwest Review.*
First published in the United Kingdom by William Heinemann, London

Book design by Paul Randall Mize

ISBN 0-385-47392-3

For Melanie Jackson

Contents

Women and Ghosts

Ilse's House

SURE, I'M AWARE that people still theorize about why I never married Gregor Spiegelman. I can understand that; Greg was a madly eligible man: good-looking, successful, charming, sexy. He reminded me of those European film stars of the thirties you see on TV reruns; he had that same suave low-key style. And then not only was he chairman of the department, he was important in his field. Everyone agreed that there were only two people in the world who knew as much as he did about Balkan economic history—some said only one.

Whereas I was just a fairly attractive young woman with a good job as a market-research analyst. It seemed kind of a fluke that I should have caught Greg, when so many had tried and failed. Women had been after him for years, ever since his marriage ended and his wife went back to Europe. I was rather pleased myself. Though I didn't let on to anyone, privately I thought Dinah Kieran was about the lucki-est girl in upstate New York.

Of course some of my friends thought Greg was way too old for me. But he didn't look anywhere near fifty-four. His springy light-brown hair was scarcely grey at all, and he was really fit: he played squash and ran two miles every day. I didn't see why his chronological age should bother me. Back in the past it used to be regarded as a coup to marry a man who was already established, instead of tak-ing a chance on some untried boy like my poor old Ma did, to her lifelong regret.

A couple of people I knew said Greg was a male chauvin-ist, but I couldn't see it. I wasn't exactly a feminist then anyhow. Sure, I was for equal rights and equal pay; I was making as much as any man in my department, and I'd had to fight for that. But when one of my girlfriends started complaining about how having a chair pulled out for her in a restaurant was insulting, I got really bored. Holy God, why shouldn't a guy treat a woman with courtesy and con-sideration if he felt like it?

I rather liked being Greg's little darling, if you want to know the truth. I liked it when he helped me into my coat and gave me a secret squeeze as he settled it round me. I liked having him bring me old-fashioned presents: expen-sive perfume and flowers and sexy lingerie in the anemone colors that go best with my black-Irish looks: red and lav-ender and hot pink. I suppose he spoiled me, really, but after the kind of childhood I had there was a lot to make up for.

When we split some people blamed it on the age differ-ence, and others said I wasn't intellectual enough for Gregor, or mature enough. Or they said our backgrounds were too different; what that meant was that I grew up in a trailer camp and didn't attend the right schools. Well, it ended so suddenly, that always makes talk. The date had been announced, the wedding invitations sent out, the caterer hired, the university chapel reserved— And then, two weeks before the ceremony, kaflooey, the whole thing was off.

In fact I was the one who broke it off. Everybody knew that, we didn't make a secret of it, and the reason we gave was the real one in a way; that I didn't want to live in Greg's house. People thought that was completely nuts, since I'd been more or less living there for months.

Greg didn't usually let on that I claimed his kitchen was haunted, because in his view that was just a crazy excuse. After all, I might not be an academic, as he said once, but I wasn't an ignorant uneducated person. I had a master's in statistics and ought to be more rational than most women, not less. He never believed I'd really seen anything. Nobody else had had any funny experiences there, not even his hippie cleaning lady, who believed in astrology and past lives.

You've got to understand, there was nothing intrinsically spooky about Greg's house. It was the kind of place you see in ads for paint and lawn care; a big white modern Colonial, on a broad tree-lined street in Corinth Heights. Ma would have died for it. Greg bought it when he got married, and the kitchen had been totally redone before his wife left. It was a big room with lots of cupboards and all the top-of-the-line equipment anyone could want: two ovens, microwave, disposal, dishwasher, you name it. It had avocado-green striped-and-flowered wallpaper, and the stove and fridge and cupboards and counters were that same pale sick green. Not my favorite color, and it was kind of dark in the daytime, because of the low ceiling and the pine trees growing so close. Still, it was just about the last place you'd expect to meet a ghost.

But I did see something. At least I thought I saw something. What I thought I saw was Ilse Spiegelman, Greg's ex-wife. Of course that didn't make any sense, because how could Ilse be a ghost if she wasn't dead? And as far as I knew she was alive and well back in Czechoslovakia, or as well as you could be under the government they had then, and teaching at the university where Greg had met her.

She was probably better off there, he said. She'd liked his house, but she never cared much for the rest of America. Even after eight years she hadn't really adjusted.

"I blame myself," he told me once. "I didn't think enough about what I was doing, taking a woman away from her country, her family, her career. I only thought of how narrow and restricted Ilse's life was. I thought of the cold cramped two-room apartment she had to share with her sister and her parents, and how she couldn't afford a warm winter coat or the books and journals she needed for her research. I imagined how happy and grateful she would be here; but I was wrong."

Greg said that naturally he'd expected Ilse would soon learn English. He was born in Europe himself and only came to America when he was ten, though you'd never know it. But Ilse wasn't good at languages, and she never got to the point where she was really comfortable in English, which made a problem when she started looking for work. Eventually she found a couple of temporary research jobs, and she did some part-time cataloguing for the library; but it wasn't what she wanted or was used to.

After a while Ilse didn't even try to find a job, Greg said, and she didn't make many friends. She wasn't as adaptable as he'd thought. In fact she turned out to be a very tense, stubborn, high-strung person, and rather selfish. When things didn't go exactly as she liked she became touchy and withdrawn.

For instance, he said, Ilse got so she didn't want to go places with him. A concert was possible, or a film, especially if it was in some language she knew. But she didn't like parties. She claimed that people talked so fast she couldn't understand them, and that they didn't want to speak to her anyhow: she was only invited because she was Gregor's wife. Everyone would be happier if she didn't go, she insisted.

When Ilse stayed home she wasn't happy either, because she imagined Greg was flirting with other women at the party. I could sort of understand how she got that idea. Greg liked women and was comfortable with them. He had a way of standing close to someone attractive and lowering his voice and speaking to her with this little quiet smile. Sometimes he would raise just his left eyebrow. It wasn't deliberate; he couldn't actually move the right one, because of a bicycle accident he'd had years ago; but it was devastating.

The way he talked to women even bothered me a bit at first, though I told myself it didn't mean anything. But it made Ilse really tense and touchy. Though she must have known what a gregarious person Greg naturally was, she started trying to get him to decline invitations. And when he did persuade her to go to some party, he told me, she followed him around, holding tight to his arm. And she always wanted to leave before he did. Well, of course that wasn't much fun for either of them, so it's no wonder if after a while Greg stopped trying to persuade her to come along.

When he went out alone, he said, Ilse would always wait up for him, even though he'd asked her over and over again not to. Then while she was waiting she'd open a bottle of liqueur, Amaretto or crème de menthe or something like that, and start sipping, and by the time he came home she'd be woozy and argumentative. When Greg told her it worried him to think of her drinking alone, Ilse got hysterical. "You have drink, at your party, why should I not have drink?" she shouted. And when Greg pointed out to her that she had finished nearly a whole bottle of Kahlúa that had been his Christmas present from his graduate students, she screamed at him and called him a tightwad, or whatever the Czech word for that is.

Finally one evening Greg came home at about one-thirty A.M. It was completely innocent, he told me: he'd been involved in a discussion about politics and forgotten the time. At first he thought Ilse had gone to sleep, but she wasn't in the bedroom and didn't answer when he called. He was worried, and went all round the house looking for her. Finally he went into the kitchen and turned on the light and saw her sitting on the floor, wedged into the space between the refrigerator and the wall where the brooms and mops were kept.

Greg said he asked her what she was doing there. I could hear just how his voice would have sounded: part anxious, part irritated, part jokey. But Ilse wouldn't answer.

"So what did you do?" I said.

"Nothing." Greg shrugged.

"Nothing?" I repeated. I didn't think he would have lost his temper, because he never did; only sometimes when he was disappointed in someone or something he'd give them this kind of cold tight look. I expected he would have looked at Ilse like that, and then hauled her out of there and helped her upstairs.

"What could I do, darling? I knew she'd been drinking and wanted to make a scene, even though she knew how much I dislike scenes. I went upstairs and got ready for bed, and after I was almost asleep I heard her come in and fall into the other bed. Next morning she didn't apologize or say anything about what had happened, and I thought it would be kinder not to bring it up. But that was when it became clear to me that it wasn't going to work out for Ilse here."

The next time I was alone in Greg's house I went into the kitchen and looked at the space between the fridge and the wall. It didn't seem wide enough for anyone to sit in. But when I pushed the brooms and mops and vacuum back and tried it myself I discovered that there was just barely enough room. I felt weird in there, like a kid playing hide-and-seek who's been forgotten by the other kids. All I could see was a section of avocado-green cupboard and a strip of vinyl floor in the yellowish-green swirly seasick pattern that I'd never liked too much. The cleaning rags and the dustpan brushed against my head and neck. I wouldn't have wanted to sit there for any length of time, even if I was a kid. And I thought that anybody who did must have been in a bad way.

I think that was a mistake, trying it out, because now I had a kind of idea of how Ilse Spiegelman must have felt. But then for a while I forgot the whole thing, because Greg asked me to marry him. Up till then he had never even mentioned marriage, and neither had I. I certainly wasn't going to hint around the way he'd said his last live-in girl-friend had, or pressure him like the one before that.

That was the year there was so much excitement in the media about a survey which claimed to prove that college-educated women over thirty had just about no chance of getting married. A couple of times people said to me, Di-nah, you're a statistician, aren't you worried? Well, Jesus, of course I was worried, because I was nearly twenty-nine, but I just smiled and said that everybody in my field knew that study was really flawed technically.

By Christmas of that year, I'd begun to sense a rising curve of possibility in the relationship; but I waited and kept my cool. Then Greg told me he'd been invited to the Rockefeller Foundation Study Center on Lake Como for a month the next summer. He said he wished I could come with him, but you weren't allowed to bring anyone but a spouse. I didn't make any suggestions. When he told me how luxurious and scenic the study center was, I just said, "Oh, really?" and, "That's great."

Three days later he brought it up again, and asked me what I'd think of our getting married before he went, because he knew I'd enjoy seeing Italy and he really didn't like the idea of leaving me behind. I didn't shriek with joy and rush into his arms, though that was what I wanted to do; I just smiled and said it sounded like a fairly good idea, as long as he didn't want us to be divorced as soon as we got back, because my poor old Ma couldn't take that.

It was the next day that I saw Ilse for the first time. I still had my apartment downtown, but I was spending a lot of time at Greg's, and sleeping over most nights. I got up early on Sunday to make sausages and waffles with maple syrup, because we'd been talking about American country breakfasts a couple of days before, and he said he'd never had a good one.

It was a wet dark late-winter morning, and the kitchen windows were streaked with half-frozen rain like transparent glue. When I went into the room the first thing I noticed was what looked like somebody's legs and feet in grey tights and worn black low-heel pumps sticking out between the refrigerator and the wall. I kind of screamed, but nothing came out except a sort of gurgle. Then I took a step nearer and saw a pale woman in a dark dress sitting wedged in there.

I didn't think of Ilse. If I thought anything, I thought we must have left the back door unlocked and some miserable homeless person or schizo graduate student had got in. "Jesus Christ, what the hell!" I screeched, and backed away and turned on the light.

And then I looked again and nobody was there. All I saw was Greg's black rubber galoshes, left to drip when we'd come in from a film the night before, and his long grey wool scarf hanging from a hook by the dusters. I couldn't see how my brain had assembled these variables into the figure of a woman, but the brain does funny things sometimes.

Later, after I got my breath back, I thought of Greg's story and realized that what I'd seen or imagined was Ilse Spiegelman. I didn't like that, because it meant that Greg's ex-wife was on my mind to an extent I hadn't suspected.

I didn't say anything about it. I damn sure wasn't going to tell Greg, who said sometimes that one of the things he loved most about me, besides my naturally pointed breasts, was my well-organized mind. "You're a wonder, Dinah," he used to tell me. "Under those wild black curls, you're as clearheaded as any man I ever met." Like a lot of guys his age, he believed that no matter how much education they got most women never became rational beings, and their heads were essentially full of unconnected lightweight ideas, like those little white Styrofoam bubbles they pack stereo equipment in.

So I didn't say anything to anybody. What I did was, I tried to find out what Ilse had looked like. My idea was that if she was really different from the thing I thought I'd seen, it would prove I'd had a hallucination. That wouldn't be so great, but it would be better than a ghost.

Greg didn't have any photos of Ilse as far as I knew; at least I couldn't find any around the house. When I asked him what she was like he only said she was blonde and shorter than me. Then I asked if she was pretty. He looked at me and laughed out loud and said, "Not anywhere near as pretty as you are, my lovely little cabbage."

After that I did a sample among his friends. I didn't take it too far; I didn't want people to think I was going into some type of retrospective jealous fit. So I didn't have a significant data base, and when I averaged their statements out all I got was the profile of a medium-sized woman in her early forties with dirty-blonde hair. Some said it was wavy and others said it was straight. They all agreed that she didn't have much to say, and her accent was hard to understand, but she was attractive, at least to start with. Later on, some of them said, she seemed to kind of let herself go, and toward the end she looked ill a lot of the time.

Greg's department secretary told me Ilse was slim but a little broad in the beam; but that information isn't much use if you're trying to identify somebody sitting on the floor behind a refrigerator. A couple of people said she looked "foreign," whatever that meant; and a colleague of Greg's said she had a "small sulky hot-looking mouth," but I had to discount that because he was always on the make.

Finally I decided that it could just possibly have been Ilse, but most likely it was my imagination. That was bad enough, because I'd never been the imaginative type, and I didn't like the idea that I was starting to see things, like one of Ma's superstitious old-lady neighbors.

The trouble was, though, I began to feel uncomfortable about Greg's kitchen. I didn't like going in there much anymore; and I always made sure to switch on the overhead light first, even if it was a bright day. I had the theory that if the light was on I wouldn't think I saw Ilse Spiegelman, and in fact I didn't.

WEEKS WENT BY, and my weird feeling about the kitchen should have gone away, only somehow it hung on. So one day I asked Greg casually what he thought of our moving after we were married. We'd been to a cocktail party at my boss's new house on the lake. It had a big fieldstone fireplace and sliding glass doors onto a deck and a really super view. I said I'd love to live in a place like that. I think it was the first time I ever asked Greg to do anything more for me than stop at the store for a bottle of Chardonnay on his way home. Up to then he'd more or less anticipated my every wish.

Well, Greg didn't see the point of it, and from a practical view there was no point. His house was in good condition, and its location was ideal: less than a mile from the university, so that on most days he could walk to his office. He said that for one thing it would be a real drag for both of us to drive to town in the kind of weather they have here from December through March. Then he reminded me how much work he'd done on his garden and grounds over the years. Next year his asparagus bed would be bearing for the first time. I wouldn't want to miss that, he said, and laughed and kissed me.

So I let it pass. By that time I'd just about convinced myself that I hadn't seen anything.

THEN ONE DAY in March I came in after work with two bags of groceries and set them on the counter and turned, and Holy Mother of God, there she was again, squeezed in by the refrigerator. It was nearly dark out, and darker inside, but I knew it was the same woman: the hair like frayed rope, the shapeless dress and shiny grey tights and black clunky pumps, scuffed at the toes, sticking out into the room.

She didn't seem to see me. She wasn't looking in my direction anyhow, but down at the seasick-green floor, just sitting there, not moving, as if she were drunk or stunned. It was much worse than the first time. Then I was just surprised and uneasy, the way anyone would be if they found a strange woman in their kitchen, but now I was like really terrified.

I almost couldn't breathe, but somehow I stumbled back and put on the light, and when I looked round she'd disappeared again. But I was sure I'd seen someone, and I was practically sure it had been Ilse. And what was worse, I got the idea that she'd been sitting there on the floor for a long while. Or maybe she was always sitting there, only most of the time I couldn't see her.

I can tell you I was in a bad state. I figured either I'd seen a ghost, or I was losing my mind. But I didn't feel crazy, except whenever I had to go into the kitchen I panicked. The main idea I had was that I had to leave that house.

Next day at breakfast I brought up moving again, but I didn't get anywhere. Greg made all the points he'd made before, and also he mentioned the financial aspects for the first time. It turned out he had no savings to speak of and not much equity in the house. But he had an eight-percent mortgage; he couldn't possibly get that kind of rate again, he said. I was a little surprised that Greg didn't have more net worth, but it made sense when I thought about it. He liked to live well: trips to New York and to conferences all over the world, expensive food and liquor, and a new Volvo every five years.

He assumed the issue was settled, but I didn't want to let it drop. I said I was making enough money to help out, and I had some savings besides; and I knew I'd be happier in a new place. Greg lowered his newspaper for a moment and glanced up at me, and for the first time I saw, just for a second, that thin cold look he gave people and things he didn't like.

But then Greg smiled slowly and folded the newspaper and put it down and came over and kissed me and said I mustn't ever worry about money. He wouldn't think of touching my little savings, he said; he had plenty for both of us.

I kissed him back, of course, and felt all warm and loved again, but at the same time just for a moment I remembered something a friend of mine at work had said when I first started going out with Greg. "He's a really sweet guy until you cross him," she said. "Then, watch out."

IN A COUPLE OF DAYS I'd more or less forgotten about that look Greg had flashed at me; but I realized I'd stuck myself with Ilse's kitchen, and my morale slid way down the chart. I didn't know what the hell to do. If I said anything to anybody they'd think I was nuts, and maybe they'd be right. Maybe I ought to just drive up to the state hospital and turn myself in. I thought of telling Ma; she believed in ghosts, and a couple of her friends had seen them; but those were always ghosts of the dead.

Then I remembered something I read in an anthropology book in college. There were sorcerers in Mexico and Central America, it said, that could project an image of themselves to anywhere they chose. The author hadn't seen it done herself, but all the locals were convinced it could happen. Well, I thought, it could be. There were some weird things in the world. Maybe Ilse Spiegelman was some kind of Czechoslovakian witch, and if she wanted to keep me from marrying Greg and moving into her house and her kitchen she might do it that way. The distance wouldn't faze her—for that kind of project two thousand miles was the same as two yards.

If I told Ma, she'd probably say I should go to a priest and ask for an exorcism. But I knew if I did that he'd give me a lot of grief for not having been to confession for three years, and living in sin with Greg. And besides, how the hell could I ask Greg to have his kitchen exorcised? I considered trying to sneak a priest into the house when Greg was at the university, but I decided it was too risky.

So I told myself okay, let's assume it was Ilse, trying to scare me off. Well, I wouldn't let her. The next time she appeared I'd make the sign of the cross and tell her to get the hell out and leave me alone. Listen, sister, I'd tell her, you had your chance with Greg, now it's my turn.

After that, instead of praying I wouldn't see Ilse I actually tried to catch her at it. For a couple of weeks, whenever Greg went out, I set my jaw and said a Hail Mary and marched into the room. I never saw a damn thing. Then, late one evening after I'd rinsed our coffee mugs in the sink and turned out the light and was leaving the kitchen, I saw her again, sitting shadowy by the refrigerator. I wasn't expecting her, so I screamed out, "Jesus Christ!"

Greg had gone up to bed already, and he heard me and called out, "What's the matter, darling?" I was frightened and confused, and I called back, "Nothing. I just cut my hand on the bread knife." Then I switched on the light, and of course nobody was there.

I thought, Oh God. That's what she wanted. She's never going to appear when I'm ready for her; she wants to surprise me, and hurt me. And now she had, because of course then I had to get out the bread knife and saw a hole in my hand to show Greg.

After that I was in a bad way. I didn't want to see Ilse when I wasn't expecting her; but I couldn't think of her the whole time. Plus I was developing a full-blown phobia about her kitchen. So I came right out and told Greg that there were things I didn't like about his house.

He was very sweet and sympathetic. He put his arms round me and kissed one of his favorite places—the back of my neck just above the left shoulder, where I have a circle of freckles. Then he asked me to tell him what it was I didn't like, and maybe it could be fixed. "I want you to be perfectly happy here, Dinah my love," he said.

Well, I told him there were three things. I said I'd like the downstairs bathroom repapered, because I'd never cared for goldfish, they had such stupid expressions; and I'd like a deck by the dining room so that we could eat outdoors in the summer. "If that's what you want, why not?" Greg said, holding me and stroking me.

Then I said I'd also like a new cabinet built in the

kitchen, between the refrigerator and the wall. That was the only thing I really cared about, because I thought that if there weren't any space there Ilse couldn't come and sit in it; and that was the only thing Greg objected to. If we put a cabinet there, he said, where would I keep my cleaning equipment? Well, I told him I'd move it out to the back entry. No, I didn't think that would be inconvenient, I said; anyhow I'd always thought a kitchen looked messy if there were old brooms and rags hanging around. I was terrified that he'd suggest building a broom cupboard, which would have been worse than nothing, but luckily it didn't occur to him.

"You want your kitchen just like your graphs, all squared away," Greg said. "All right, darling." And he laughed. He liked to tease me sometimes about my passion for order.

Greg promised to have the improvements made before the wedding, and he carried through. The day the new cabinet was installed I went into the kitchen the minute I got home. Just as I'd planned, it completely filled the space where Ilse had sat. There was a drawer under the counter, and a shelf under that; nobody could possibly get in there. I stooped down and looked to make sure, and then I put in a couple of baking tins and some bags of paper cups and plates.

I've done it, I thought, and I was really happy. I thought how generous and brilliant and good-looking Greg was, and how smart I was, and how we were going to Montreal for our honeymoon and then to Europe. I'd bought a beautiful wedding dress: heavy ecru silk with a sexy low square neck and yards of lace.

WELL, IT GOT TO BE two weeks before the wedding. I was so high I was even starting to feel a little sorry for Ilse. I thought about how she was probably back in those two nasty little rooms again with her family. I knew what that was like, from the years I spent with my mother and sisters in the trailer camp, with cold sour air leaking through the window frames and the kitchen faucet spitting rust and the neighbors playing the radio or screaming at each other all night. No wonder she was jealous.

Then the term was nearly over, and Greg's department was giving a reception. He called me that Friday afternoon from his office to say they were short of paper plates and could I drop some by after work? So when I got home I went into the kitchen and opened the new cabinet by the refrigerator.

It was a good thing I was alone, because I let out a real burglar-alarm screech. There was Ilse Spiegelman, just like before, only now she was shrunken down into some kind of horrible little dwarf about two and a half feet high. I didn't even try the light, I just howled and stumbled out into the hall.

It took me nearly thirty-five minutes to get up my nerve to go back into the kitchen—where of course Ilse wasn't anymore, or at least I couldn't see her—and put my hand into that cabinet, maybe right through her, and take out those paper plates that Greg was waiting for.

After that I knew I was beaten. If Ilse could shrink herself like that she could appear any size, and anywhere she goddamn wanted to. Maybe she'd get into the flour bin in the pantry next, or maybe someday when I took the lid off the top of the sugar bowl she'd be in there, all squnched up.

I was really depressed and sort of desperate. But then I thought that maybe Ilse wouldn't mind my living with Greg as long as we weren't married. After all, she hadn't even appeared until we got engaged.

So that evening I told Greg I didn't think I could go through with it. I said I was terrified of the responsibility of marriage. At first he was wonderful. He held me and kissed me and petted me and said that was perfectly natural: mar-

riage *was* frightening. And of course, he added, I was probably apprehensive about becoming a department chairman's wife.

"Yeah, that's right," I said, though that thought hadn't
occurred to me.

He understood, Greg said. I might not think I was up to
the job, but he would help me; and if anybody tried to
make me feel incompetent or not worthy of him, he would
give them hell.

When I kept on insisting that I didn't want to get married, Greg asked what had changed my mind. I was still
afraid to tell him about Ilse; I didn't want him to think I'd
gone off the deep end. So I came up with the kind of stuff
you read everywhere those days about marriage being an
outmoded patriarchal contract, and how the idea of own-
ing another human being was fascist. I probably didn't
make a very good presentation, because I didn't believe in
what I was saying. Anyhow, Greg didn't buy it.

"You surprise me, Dinah," he said, raising his left eyebrow. "I've never heard you talk like this before. Who's
been brainwashing you, I wonder?"

Well, I swore nobody had. I burbled on, saying I loved
him so much, but I was frightened, and why couldn't we
just go on the way we were? After all, I said, he'd been with
other women and he hadn't wanted to marry them. That
was a mistake. Greg's face changed, and he gave me that
bad look again. Then he dropped his arm and sort of
pushed me aside.

"What is this?" he said, laughing in an unfriendly way.
"The revenge of the bimbos?"

"Huh?" I was completely at a loss; but finally I got what
he meant. There were maybe four or five women in town
who had wanted to marry Greg, and some of them were
still pretty hurt and angry according to rumor. He meant,
was I doing it for them?

"Jesus no," I said. "I don't owe those women anything. They're none of them my friends." Then he seemed convinced and quieted down.

But I still said I didn't want to get married. Greg tried to reassure me some more, but I could see he was getting impatient. He asked if I realized that if I broke off our engagement it would embarrass him in front of everyone and make him a local joke. He'd already had to take some kidding from friends because he'd sworn so often that he was never going to marry again. And there were quite a few people on campus who weren't Greg's friends: people who envied his success and would have loved for him to mess up somehow.

I felt awful about that, and I said he could blame it all on me: he could tell everybody I was being silly and neurotic. But Greg explained that this would be almost as bad, because people would think less of him for having a relationship with someone like that.

Then he sat back and looked at me in that hard considering way, as if I was a student who'd plagiarized a paper or some article he didn't approve of, and finally he said slowly, "There's something else behind this, Dinah. And I can take a guess at what it is."

What it turned out to be was, Greg thought I must have got involved with somebody else, probably some guy nearer my own age, only I was afraid to admit it. I swore there wasn't anybody. I kept saying I loved him, that he was the only person I loved, but he didn't seem to hear me anymore. He pushed his face up close to mine so it filled my whole visual field and looked all distorted, like something you see in the previews of a horror film for a split second: not long enough to be sure what it is, but long enough to know it's something awful.

"All right, who is it, you bitch? Who?" he shouted, and when I kept saying "Nobody," he took hold of me and shook me as if I were a bottle of ketchup and he could shake out some man's name. Only there wasn't any name.

When Greg let go, and I could stop trembling and crying, I told him the truth, only he didn't believe me. Instead he started going over all the other explanations he'd thought up. Gradually things got really strange and scary. Greg was cursing in this tight hard voice and saying that if I really thought I'd seen Ilse sitting in the kitchen cabinet I must be going crazy; and I was weeping. I said that if I were going crazy it would be wicked of me to marry him and ruin his life, and he said I already had.

It went on like that all weekend. We hardly slept, and finally I got so miserable and mixed up and exhausted that I started agreeing with everything Greg said. That I had probably been brainwashed by feminists, and that I was sometimes attracted to younger men; and that I was basically irrational, deceptive, cowardly, neurotic, and unconsciously envious of Greg because he was a superior person and I was nobody to speak of. The weird thing was that I didn't just agree to all this; in the state I was in by then, I'd started to believe whatever he said.

On Monday morning we were in the kitchen trying to have breakfast. I was in really bad shape; I hadn't had a bath or done anything about my hair for two days, and over my nightgown I had on an old red terry-cloth bathrobe with coffee stains. I had got to the point where I didn't care anymore if I was crazy or not. I thought that if Ilse Spiegelman meant to haunt me for the rest of my life it couldn't be worse than this.

So when Greg came downstairs I told him I wanted to forget the whole thing and go ahead with the wedding. I put two pieces of Pepperidge Farm raisin toast on his plate, and he looked at them. And then he looked at me, and I could see that he didn't want to marry me anymore, and also he didn't want to live with me.

I was right, too. Later that morning Greg called my office and said that he thought it would be best if we didn't see each other or speak to each other again. So he was putting all my "debris" out in the back entry, and would I please collect it before 6 P.M.?

WELL, AFTER WORK I went round. I could tell how upset and furious Greg still was by the way he'd pitched my belongings out the kitchen door. My lavender nightgown looked as if it had been strangled, and there was raisin granola spilled everywhere; and a bottle of conditioner that he hadn't bothered to close had leaked over everything. It was a total mess. All the time I was cleaning it up I was crying and carrying on, because I still thought I was in love with Greg and that everything that had happened was my fault. And I couldn't help it, I didn't want to, but I looked through the glass of the kitchen door once more to see if Ilse was there. Maybe she would be smiling now, I thought, or even laughing. The cabinet door was hanging open, but it was empty.

I piled everything into the car and drove to my apartment; thank God, the lease still had a month to run. But the place looked awful. I'd hardly been there for weeks, and there was dust everywhere and the windows were grimed over with soot. I managed to unload the car and carry everything upstairs, and dumped a heap of clothes sticky with conditioner and granola into the bathtub, and knelt down to turn on the water.

Then it really hit me. I felt so defeated and crazy and miserable that I slid down onto the dirty yellow vinyl and sat there in a heap between the tub and the toilet. I felt like killing myself, but I didn't have enough energy to move. I thought that maybe in a little while I would crawl across the floor and put my head in the gas oven.

Then all of a sudden I realized that I was sitting on the

floor in a cramped space, just like Ilse. She'd finally reduced me to her own miserable condition.

But maybe she wasn't the only one who had done that, I thought. And for the first time I wondered if Greg had ever said the kind of things to Ilse he'd been saying to me all weekend, till she blamed herself for everything and was totally wiped out and beaten down. I remembered how his face had turned into a horror-film preview, and suddenly I felt kind of lucky to have got out of his house. I thought that even if he changed his mind now and took me back, and was as charming and affectionate as before, I would always remember this weekend and wonder if it would happen again, and I would have to sort of tiptoe round him for the rest of my life.

What if I was wrong to believe Ilse had been trying to stop me marrying Greg? I thought. What if she had been trying to warn me?

I still don't know for sure if that's right. Now that everything's changed over there, I'd really like to go to Czechoslovakia and look her up and ask her. But I don't see how I can, what with my husband and the baby.

Gregor's never married again, though he's been with a lot of different women since we separated. I wonder sometimes if any of them have seen Ilse. But maybe she hasn't had to appear, because none of his relationships seem to last very long.

The Pool
People

CLARY GRABER'S HUSBAND had warned her against
staying with his mother for three weeks, but Clary decided to go to Key West that April anyhow. She was determined to get four-year-old Kate out of grey drizzling Boston. Her daughter had had a runny, wet cold off and on
ever since Christmas, and a worrying little cough. It was
dreadful to see her snuffling around the apartment day after
day, pale and limp and whiny, not her normal self at all.
But outdoors, in the sun . . .

"Sure, it might help," Ron said. "But you're going to be
irritated and bored out of your mind down there, darling."

"I don't see why; we all had a good time last year," said
Clary, who sometimes congratulated herself on her ability
to get on with her mother-in-law, unlike many of her married friends.

"Yeah," Ron grinned. "For four days."

"And I think it was really nice of June to invite us."

Clary didn't mention that she'd suggested the visit herself. "Besides, you're going to be in Brussels most of next month."

"Okay, if that's what you want."

EVEN AFTER A WEEK in Key West, during which she often had to admit that Ron had had a point, Clary knew she'd been right to come. Kate's sniffles had dried up almost overnight, and in a few days the cough was gone too and she was full of energy and joy. It was marvelous to watch her in June's pool, paddling about at the shallow end in her ruffled swimsuit and orange life jacket, sailing leaves or a yellow plastic boat full of plastic Ninja Turtles.

It was the first time that either Clary or Kate had really swum there. Ron always insisted on going to the beach; he didn't care for his mother's pool. It was an unusual shape: long and trapezoidal, and Ron said that when he did laps he kept banging into the sides. He disliked the noise of the pool machinery, and the way the water bulged and seethed and churned below the surface at the deep end, as if it were coming to a boil. It gave him a queasy feeling, exactly like June's cooking, he said.

Clary saw absolutely nothing wrong with June's pool. Because it was so deep, and heavily shaded most of the day, it hadn't become stale and warm at the end of the season. The water remained limpidly cool, with a shifting pattern in its depths, white reflections on aquamarine like delicate wire netting. Its constant flow was silky, sensual, caressing; and the hum of the filter peaceful, almost soporific. Clary thought that what Ron had really wanted, as usual, was to get away from his mother.

Ever since they'd met, Clary had felt sorry for June Graber. Some people might have said that was ridiculous, because June was healthy and remarkably attractive for fifty-eight, and she was also extremely well off, having been married to three very rich men. But you had to feel sorry for somebody whose son made jokes about her behind her back and who didn't appear to have any real friends.

It was true, June knew a lot of people in Key West, but she didn't seem to know them very well. According to articles Clary had read, the town was supposed to be full of interesting types, but June didn't seem to have met any of them. Her acquaintances were all well-to-do retired people, mildly and monotonously interested in travel, real estate, home improvement, tropical gardening, and their own ailments. These people also had less than no interest in children; they tended to become anxious as soon as they saw Kate. It was written all over their faces that they were afraid she would damage their rice-paper screens or their hand-blown crystal, or that Kate herself would be injured by their spoilt and irritable pets. Of course it would have been more sensible to leave Kate at home with a sitter, but in Key West during the season sitters were a vanished species; all the local teenagers were working in shops or restaurants.

After a couple of disastrous encounters, Clary decided that it would be easier, not to mention less boring, to take Kate away whenever June's friends came over, and stay home when June was invited out. Kate didn't mind being alone; she carried on long conversations with her plastic turtles, and with two imaginary friends called Davy and Big Bill who lived in the pool.

Clary recognized the names, which were those of the carpenters who had been remodeling June's Key West house last year. Kate had made friends with them, following them about and feeding them animal crackers, her favorite food. Davy, who was small and dark and handsome and sometimes wore a purple T-shirt with the slogan GAY IS GOOD, told Kate long stories about his dog. Big Bill, a large, slow-moving, muscular young man with three children of his own, made her a set of blocks out of ends of lumber, carefully shaped and sanded.

Kate's current Davy and Big Bill were not exactly like the ones she had known; they were blue, and you could see right through them. Some days they were in the pool, she explained to her mother, and other days they weren't.

Clary, however, had no friends in Key West, imaginary or otherwise. The only adults she had spoken to now in days besides her mother-in-law were Rusty and Joy, two handsome, deeply tanned, slightly spacey Key Westerners who came twice a week to clean and service the pool.

But she was reconciled to being bored. A more serious disappointment was her mother-in-law's lack of interest in Kate. June had always been, or pretended to be, dotingly fond of her granddaughter, and Clary had assumed she'd want to spend time with her. She had imagined how, during this time, she herself would be exploring the shops and art galleries, or out on the reef, snorkeling through a cool pale-green universe of brilliantly hued coral and sparkling fish. Instead, she literally couldn't go anywhere alone.

"It's so long since I had a small child," June had explained when Clary first suggested that she might take Kate somewhere. "I'd feel much more comfortable if you came along too."

Another thing that Clary hadn't fully realized was that her mother-in-law was a compulsive talker; she had thought of her, simply, as lively and voluble. But in the past there'd always been other listeners around; now Clary was the only one. The moment June entered the room she began a monologue, even if Clary was reading to Kate or watching the news on TV. She followed her daughter-in-law from room to room, out to the pool and back, talking and talking, and if Clary was going anywhere June always volunteered to come along.

The only time June was quiet was during and just after

her daily swim. She did laps every morning for twenty minutes in a silvery or aqua dressmaker suit, her carefully streaked and set gold hair bunched under a white rubber cap, her leathery bronze shoulders glistening. When she came out and lay dripping on one of the chaise lounges she seemed for a little while to be a different person, with a different, peaceful, sated expression.

"Oh, that felt wonderful," she might murmur, or "I wish I could stay in the water forever." Then for up to fifteen minutes she would lie silent, her eyes closed.

Occasionally June spoke of films or TV programs, but her usual topics were goods and services. Each morning she drove back and forth across the island in her rented Buick Le Sabre with the air-conditioning turned to high, prowling the end-of-season sales. She returned at lunchtime with news of reconnaissance, attack, skirmish, and defeat or triumph in her battle for the most desirable food, drink, clothing, and household furnishings and services. ("Would you believe it, there's not such a thing as a down cushion/salad spinner/scissor sharpener on this entire island. . . . I tried Sears first, and this absolutely imbecile salesgirl said she'd never heard of them. And then I went to Strunk's, I'm positive I saw some there last year, only the man denied it. . . . He was incredibly rude, and I told him so, I said . . .")

June's most extended narrative concerned the remodeling of her house. Its basic theme was the delay, deception, and waste of expensive materials that had taken place during construction. These were, June declared in a favorite phrase, "mind-boggling." ("I used to wonder, when I was a kid, you know, how you boggled a mind," Ron had remarked once. "I figured you did it with some kind of mechanical gizmo, kind of like a toggle switch." Clary hadn't laughed; she'd had her own troubles with workmen.)

Now she heard the saga again, with additions and elaborations. There'd been nothing but trouble from the first, according to June. The job had been delayed literally for months because of objections from Historic Preservation of Key West, and their ridiculous rules about everything from the colors of paint you could use to the seven feet you were supposed to leave on each side of your lot, though half the houses in town were jammed up smack against the property line. But if you were a local, as far as June could see, whatever you wanted to build was just fine. She got so furious at one point that she threatened to sue Historic Preservation, which she might as well have done, because after her lawyer talked her out of it the old biddies on the board raised even more objections, and her architect had to redraw the plans at a frightful cost (figures supplied).

Several times during the summer June had had to come down to keep an eye on things.

"The heat was frightful, totally exhausting, but I truly believe that if I hadn't been here they would never have lifted a finger," she announced. It was just after lunch and she was sitting by the patio table, chain-smoking, while Clary tried to read the *Times* and Kate, humming softly to herself, colored a paper napkin. Overhead high shredded clouds drifted across a pale light-suffused sky; leaves rustled down one by one from the banyan and sapodilla trees; and the bare blunt fingers of the frangipani invisibly unfolded sprays of creamy stars.

"You cannot picture how slowly they were working," June continued, breaking the calm.

"Mm," Clary said. In fact she could picture it. Key West was a leisurely, laid-back place: the speed limit, even on the highway to the airport, was thirty-five miles an hour. June Graber, however, was used to life on the fast track. She didn't decelerate in Key West; maybe, after nearly sixty years in Manhattan, she didn't know how.

"Of course the contractor was never around when I wanted him," she told Clary, stubbing out her Kent and lighting another, "and those two carpenters of his were impossible. Half the time they were just pretending to be working. I'd look out of the window and I'd see Big Bill carrying a piece of pipe around the side of the house, and five minutes later I'd see him carrying the same pipe back.

"And then, if I asked that big good-looking oaf what he thought he was doing, he wouldn't answer. It turned out he had a hearing problem, but even when I came up close and positively shouted he just kept nodding stupidly and repeating 'Yes, ma'am. Right you are, ma'am.' And on top of that, he was a born-again Christian. For a while he was actually trying to convert me." June laughed shrilly. "He kept leaving these smarmy evangelistic tracts around the house, and once he told me that if I would let Christ into my heart I would find peace. Can you imagine the nerve?"

"Mm," said Clary. I wish to God you *would* find peace, she thought, and then, ashamed of herself, added, "Awfully annoying."

"Awfully. And I very soon found out I had to watch them every minute, or else something was sure to go wrong. Well, for example, one day I was having a sprout sandwich here on the deck, and I glanced up and saw that Davy—you remember him, that tough-looking little homosexual—was getting far more paint on my aralias than he was on my fence." June indicated the leggy, rustling shrubs that edged her backyard.

"The contractor had asked me please not to talk to the crew, to come to him if I had any problem. But really, he was never there half the time, and if I saw somebody doing something stupid right under my nose, I was going to mention it. I had no intention of paying for sloppy work and the waste of expensive materials. That's exactly what I said."

"Yes, I remember your telling me," prompted Clary, hoping to urge June toward the end of this familiar episode.

"So when I saw that Davy simply splashing paint everywhere, naturally I spoke up. I said I'd never seen such carelessness. I'd been watching him for fifteen minutes, I said, and he wasn't worth sixteen dollars an hour. Well, I don't know if I told you—"

"You told me," Clary murmured.

"—he became incredibly offensive. At first he didn't even answer me, he simply slammed down his wet paintbrush right on the tiles, you can still see the mark if you move that pincushion cactus, and stood up and started to walk away.

"So naturally I followed him. 'Where do you think you're going?' I asked, but really quite calmly and nicely. 'I'm paying you for your time,' I said, 'and I'd really like you to listen when I speak to you.' Well, then Davy turned round. He pulled his arm away and screamed at me. 'Oh, go to hell, lady!' he positively screamed." June looked at Clary for a reaction.

"Very rude," she said, feeling as if she were repeating lines in a play.

"Yes. That's exactly what he said, shouted really, and then he climbed on his motorbike and rode off. Can you imagine?"

"Mm," Clary said. If only June would stop talking for just a moment, she thought. And we'll be here for nearly two more weeks.

"Well, of course I was furious. I told my contractor he had to fire Davy, but he persuaded me to give him another chance. What a mistake that was, but I guess I have a soft heart." June placed her manicured hand on washed aquamarine silk above the relevant spot.

"Of course, after Davy came back he was terribly sulky for a while, but I tried to overlook it. And then later I found out he'd had the nerve to tell people *he'd* decided to give *me* another chance, because I was obviously under the influence of negative forces from some previous-life personality.

"Absolutely. He said that. He was one of those New Age types; he always wore a crystal round his neck on a chain." June made the same face she had made at a restaurant the night before over some doubtful soft-shell crabs. "My private opinion is, they were probably all three of them on drugs."

"Mm." Clary raised and turned the pages of the *Times*, but June didn't take the hint.

"Right before I left for New York in July," she continued, "I came back to the house unexpectedly at lunchtime, and what did I see?"

"Yes, I know, you saw—"

"Just let me tell you," June interrupted. "I saw Big Bill sitting on the edge of my pool, dangling his beefy legs in the water and eating a sloppy-joe sandwich. Davy was there too, lying beside him smoking, and his long greasy hair was wet, which proved that he had been swimming.

"Well, I made a big effort: I controlled myself and didn't say anything till I saw Mac, and then I told him I'd prefer it if the crew didn't eat on the job or use my pool. Just that, very politely. I didn't contradict him when he pretended they hadn't been swimming, or say anything about not wanting bits of bread and tomatoes and cigarette ashes and long greasy hair in the water I swam in every day. I think that was perfectly reasonable," June finished, on a note of inquiry.

"Mm, certainly," Clary agreed, looking at the pool as it rocked in the sun-dappled shade like a cool, pure trapezoid of ice-blue Perrier.

"But that's the kind of help you get down here." June sighed. "The cleaner we had last winter . . ."

Briefly June was diverted, but soon she resumed the saga of the house. After she went back to New York, she said, everything began to go wrong. She could tell from the photos—thank God she had absolutely demanded photos with the weekly statement. The bedroom windows had four panes instead of nine, and the closet shelf divider was completely off center, and they'd used this hideous grey grout between the salmon-pink tiles in the bathroom and hung the mirror horizontally instead of vertically. Naturally she insisted that everything be done over.

"And then, can you believe it, Mac expected me to pay for their errors. It simply didn't make sense. I sometimes think that he was deliberately allowing things to go wrong, maybe subconsciously. A friend of mine, she's a therapist, and she said it sounded to her like Mac was a passive-aggressive personality who was working out his hostility to more successful members of society by screwing up my house along with his own career."

About this time, June said, it became nearly impossible to get hold of Mac on the phone. Even if she called him at 11 P.M. after the rates went down, he'd have his machine on. Or else his wife would answer, and Clary couldn't imagine how rude *she* was. " 'Mac has to get up in six hours to work on your house, and I'm not going to wake him now for you or God herself.' That's exactly how she put it, she was some kind of feminist nut."

Clary, with difficulty, suppressed any comment; but one was supplied by Kate, who was now playing on the deck under a red hibiscus. "She goes, n' she goes, n' she goes on," Kate sang, pushing a plastic truck laden with plastic turtles along a track between two boards.

Warming to her subject, lighting another cigarette, June described the final battle. She related how she had paid to have her Key West phone turned on so she could reach Mac on the job, and how often he wasn't there. "I'd call and Big Bill or Davy would tell me that he was at the lumberyard. And then I'd call back an hour later and they'd say he was at City Hall. Well, eventually I blew up. 'God damn it,' I said, 'I'm tired of hearing your lame excuses. Do you know what these calls are costing me?' "

Perhaps predictably, when June phoned the following day her Key West number did not answer, though she tried it for over an hour, becoming more and more upset and furious. Finally she called her next-door neighbor, an elderly woman with arthritis. She was sorry to bother her, June said, but she had to know what the hell was going on at her house.

Reluctantly, the neighbor agreed to investigate. While the phone charges rapidly piled up, she went slowly next door and came slowly back to tell June that nobody was home. After further persuasion, she went out into her yard, climbed onto a bench, and looked over the wall. She returned to report that the fellows who were working over to June's place probably hadn't heard the phone or the bell on account of they were in the pool. Wishing not to cause trouble, she neglected to mention that they were in the pool without any clothes on, though this came out later.

"Yes. Buck naked, in my pool. Can you imagine?" (June spoke, it struck Clary, with a mixed thrill of horror and sexual excitement. She was reminded of something embarrassing a drunken elderly man had said to her at a Key West party a year ago: "Age calls to youth. I've got a giant crush on you, Clary, just like June's got the hots for those good-looking workmen of hers.")

As soon as she hung up, June Graber continued, she started dialing her Key West number again, and she kept at it for over two hours, until Mac finally answered.

If anything could have made the situation worse then, she said, it was his attitude. He didn't apologize or try to pretend he didn't know what had been going on; instead he laughed.

" 'For Christ's sake, Mrs. Graber,' he said. 'It's nearly ninety-five degrees out today, that's goddamn hot, and the guys were on their lunch break. Anyhow, if you're not here, what difference does it make?'

"Well, I answered that question. I said it wasn't merely that his crew had deliberately contravened my orders. He'd also allowed someone who could very well be infected with AIDS to use the pool. 'You're not going to deny that Davy is a homosexual, I suppose,' I told him.''

Mac did not try to deny this, June said. Instead, could you believe it, he started to act as if she were at fault and not him. He claimed that there was nothing wrong with Davy, and that anyhow you couldn't get AIDS from swimming in the same pool as an infected person.

" 'Yes, that's what the so-called experts tell us,' I said to him,'' June declared. " 'They tell us the water is safe to drink and the wax on apples doesn't cause cancer and a whole lot of things like that, and later you find out they were lying. I'm taking no chances,' I said.

"Well, then Mac changed his tune. 'All right,' he said to me, but very unpleasantly, you know. 'If it bothers you so much, I'll tell the guys to stay out of the pool.' ''

June took a breath, preparing for the climax. "You know what I said to him? I said, 'I don't want you to tell them anything. I want all three of you off my property this afternoon.' '' She smiled, reliving her victory. "I told him, 'I don't ever want to see you or those lazy bums you've got working for you again.' That's exactly what I said.'' She blew a self-congratulatory cloud of smoke.

Of course, June added, Mac had tried to argue with her. "But I simply wouldn't listen, though it meant I had to fly back down to Key West and find another builder (what a frightful job that was; I'll tell you all about it later). And then Mac had the gall to send in a final bill for over three thousand dollars, when I'd already paid far more than the work was worth. The way I figure it, he was lucky I didn't sue him for contaminating my pool.''

June smiled, ground out her cigarette, and looked round. "And what did you do this morning, Katie?" she called to her granddaughter.

"Played with the pool people," Kate said.

"They came today? Now that is rather annoying." June frowned. "Monday and Thursday are their days, you know, Clary, and I really can't have—"

"It's not your regular pool people she means," Clary said. "Not Rusty and Joy."

"Uh-uh," Kate agreed, walking a plastic turtle across the deck toward her grandmother. "Davy and Big Bill."

Uncharacteristically, June was silent. She had gone pale under her leathery tan, and her expression was one of strain, even panic.

"Kate hasn't really seen Davy and Big Bill, I'm sure," Clary reassured her. "She's just remembered them from last year, and used their names for her imaginary friends. You know, back home she has an imaginary rabbit. It takes baths with her. Are Davy and Big Bill rabbits too, darling?"

"Nope. Like ordinary people, 'cept they're blue."

"You see, June, they're blue." Clary laughed. "And they don't come in from the street like ordinary people, do they?"

Kate shook her head. "Live in pool," she explained, pointing downward into the water. "They said, when was my Grammy coming to swim at night again? We want to play with her. That's you," she told June. "You're my Grammy."

June sat frozen; she opened her mouth but seemed for once unable to speak. Either she disapproved of imaginary friends, Clary thought, or she was furious at Kate's term of address. She had already said several times that she didn't want to be called Grammy, Grandma, or Granny. ("It always makes me feel like some pathetic little old lady. Why can't Kate say 'June,' like everyone else in the family?")

THE FOLLOWING DAY it turned very hot, and when Rusty came to clean the pool Clary brought him iced tea.

"Thanks," he said, leaning against the shady side of the house. "Nice and peaceful here. You'd never know—" He paused.

"Never know what?"

"Well." He took another long swallow. "All that bad business last fall."

"You mean the way those workmen behaved to Mrs. Graber." No doubt everyone in town's heard that story by now, Clary thought.

Rusty gave her a hard look. "Hell, no. I mean the shitty way she behaved to them, excuse me. And what happened afterward."

"Really?" said Clary. "What happened afterward?"

"Well." He looked across the deck to where Kate was digging in a flower bed. "After she fired those guys, and wouldn't pay what she owed them—you know about that?"

"Yes," Clary said. "At least, that is—" She frowned.

"Well, they were up the creek. It wasn't so hard on Mac. He had a couple of repair jobs lined up, and some savings. But Big Bill had a wife and three children under six, and he really needed the money. So when this character he knew asked him to drive a load of never-mind-what to an address in Atlanta, for a thousand dollars, he said okay. You never heard any of this?"

"No."

"Hell, maybe I shouldn't—"

"Go on."

"Well. Okay. Big Bill, he made it the first time, but on the second trip he ran into a police roadblock just north of Summerland Key. He freaked out and turned the truck round and started back, and a couple of cops started after him. Pretty soon he got to speeding, and when he came to the construction on the bridge he lost control and crashed through a barrier and was DOA at Keys Memorial Hospital."

"Oh, that's awful." Clary set down her iced tea; her fingers felt frozen. "I'm really sorry—"

"And then Davy. You heard about that?" Clary shook her head. "He didn't have any family responsibilities, but he was paying out over eighty dollars a week for AZT. He tried to get on the county program, but they had a six-week waiting period. So he got antsy and took off for San Francisco, where he'd heard the situation was better, only he ran into more red tape there. Sold his bike and was sleeping in a park. Round about Thanksgiving he decided he couldn't take waiting around to get sick and die, so he jumped off some big building they have out there."

"Oh, awful," Clary repeated. "But I really don't think June—Mrs. Graber—knows any of this, or she wouldn't be so—" She paused, unable to think of a neutral term.

"She knows," Rusty said. "She knows, all right, because I told her when she got down here just before Christmas."

ON CLARY'S ARRIVAL in Key West, June had declared that she was going to give a cocktail party for her. Clary had thanked her mother-in-law politely, but now that the gift had been presented she wasn't enjoying it much. Under an orange-stained, rapidly fading sunset, two dozen well-preserved aging people in strangely youthful and colorful garb—fire-engine-red slacks, Hawaiian shirts, yellow Bermuda shorts, and purple ruffled sundresses—stood around the illuminated pool with drinks in their hands. As dusk fell the water glowed brighter and brighter, an almost supernatural turquoise; but they turned their backs on it, absorbed in news of local real estate transactions and their own homes, plants, pets, and ailments.

June, in pink silk patio pajamas, wove continually among her guests, urging them to try the conch fritters. Clary stood by the shallow end watching her daughter sail leaves and hibiscus flowers in the water and listening to a discussion of restaurants in Bermuda, where she had never been and had no wish to go.

Suddenly, at the other end of the pool, there was a commotion. June Graber, or so it appeared later, had taken a step backward and fallen in. There were screams and splashing, increasing to a crescendo as several of June's guests, most of them over sixty and more or less woozy with alcohol, jumped in to save her, some on top of each other.

Almost at once the slippery trapezoid of water was full of thrashing multicolored bodies, the air of confused, hysterical cries. Other guests waded in past Kate, or threw green and magenta-flowered chair cushions that, though intended as life preservers, acted as weapons.

It was fully dark when all the would-be rescuers were helped from the pool, or sloshed themselves out of it, bruised and dazed. June Graber was removed last. Apparently she had hit her head on something and sunk almost at once. Though several volunteers, and later an ambulance crew, tried to revive her, they all failed.

Clary didn't witness these vain efforts; at the first glimpse of that heavy, sodden pink thing, she had hurried Kate into the house.

BACK IN BOSTON, once the shock had worn off, Clary and Ron's main concern was for Kate. A child's first experience of death was important, and had to be handled tactfully.

"You see, darling," Clary concluded. "That's why you always have to wear your life jacket when you're around water, because you can't always be thinking about being careful all the time. Grammy wasn't thinking about it, so she walked backward and fell into the pool."

"No," Kate said.

"How do you mean, no?" Clary hugged Kate anxiously.

"Grammy didn't walk backward. Big Bill grabbed on her leg and pulled, and then Davy pushed her down in the water."

"Oh, no, honey," her father protested.

But in spite of anything her parents could say, Kate stuck to her version. When they continued to press her she burst into tears, and it took the best efforts of both Clary and Ron to calm her.

"Kate doesn't really understand about death yet; she's just too young," Clary said later. "When I put her to bed tonight she told me that your mother is living in the pool in Key West."

"She said something like that to me too," Ron agreed. "I think maybe it's just a way of denying that she'll never see June again, because the loss is still too painful."

"Ye-es." It was painful for Ron, Clary thought—far more than she would have guessed. But really June didn't mean anything to Kate. It was just as well that they had never been close.

Clary pictured June's house in Key West, now on the market, since Ron had refused to go there ever again. She could see the backyard clearly in her mind: the shutters would be closed now, the deck furniture under plastic covers. But the outside spotlights, intended to deter burglars, would have come on automatically at dusk, bathing the palms and hibiscus in their unnatural glow. And the pool would still be full; the real estate agent thought that looked better to prospective buyers.

The water is as cool and clear and silvery green as ever, Clary thought: rippling out from the inlets with the same slow silky bubbling and churning, the same low continuing hum. And there are the same leafy reflections on the surface. And the same shifting lattice patterns on the bottom—as if someone were slowly shaking a spectral net in which, down at the deep end, shadowy blue figures were moving.

The
Highboy

EVEN BEFORE I KNEW more about that piece of furniture I wouldn't have wanted it in my house. For a valuable antique, it wasn't particularly attractive: with that tall stack of dark mahogany drawers and those long spindly bowed legs, it looked not only heavy but top-heavy. But then Clark and I have never cared much for Chippendale; we prefer simple lines and light woods. The carved bonnet top of the highboy was too elaborate for my taste, and the surface had been polished till it glistened a deep blackish brown, the color of canned prunes.

Still, I could understand why the piece meant so much to Clark's sister-in-law, Buffy Stockwell. It mattered to her that she had what she called "really good things": that her antiques were genuine and her china was Spode. She never made a point of how superior her "things" were to most people's, but one was always aware of it. And besides, the highboy was an heirloom; it had been in her family for years. I could easily see why she was disappointed and cross when her aunt left it to Buffy's brother.

"I don't want to sound ungrateful, Janet, honestly," Buffy told me over lunch at the country club. "I realize Jack's carrying on the family name and I'm not. And of course I was glad to have Aunt Betsy's Tiffany coffee service. I suppose it's worth more than the highboy actually, but it just doesn't have any past. It's got no personality, if you know what I mean."

Buffy giggled, but I barely smiled. My sister-in-law was given to anthropomorphizing her possessions, speaking of them as if they had almost human traits: "A dear little Paul Revere sugar spoon." "It's lively, even kind of aggressive, for a wicker plant stand—but I think it'll be really happy on the sun porch." Whenever their washer or sit-down mower or VCR wasn't working properly she'd say it was "ill." I'd thought the habit endearing once, but by now it had begun to rather bore me.

"I don't understand it really," Buffy said, digging her little dessert fork into the lemon cream tart that she always ordered at the club after declaring—quite rightly—that she shouldn't. "After all, I'm the one who was named for Aunt Betsy, and she knew how interested I was in family history. I always thought I was her favorite. Well, live and learn." She giggled again in that rather self-consciously girlish way she had and took another bite, leaving a fleck of whipped cream on her short, pouting upper lip.

You mustn't get me wrong. Buffy and her husband Bobby, Clark's brother, were both dears, and as affectionate and reliable and nice as anyone could possibly be. But even Clark and I had to admit that they'd never quite grown up. Bobby was sixty-one and a vice president of his company, but his life still centered around golf and tennis.

Buffy, who was nearly his age, didn't play anymore because of her heart. But she still favored yellow and shocking-pink sportswear with rather silly designs. She kept her hair blonde and wore it in all-over curls, and maintained her girlish manner. Then of course she had these bouts of childlike whimsicality: she attributed opinions to their pets, and named their automobiles. As long as it was alive, she had insisted that their poodle Suzy didn't like the mailman because he was a Democrat, and for years she had had a series of Plymouth Valiant wagons called Prince.

THE NEXT TIME the subject of the highboy came up was at a big dinner party about a month later, after Buffy'd been to see her brother in Connecticut. "It wasn't all that successful a visit," she reported. "You know my Aunt Betsy Lumpkin left Jack her Newport highboy, that I was hoping would come to me. I think I told you."

I agreed that she had.

"Well, it's in his house in Stonington now," Buffy said. "But it's completely out of place there, among all that pickled walnut imitation French-provincial furniture that Jack's new wife chose, and those boring fashion plates. It looked so *uncomfortable.*" She sighed and accepted another helping of roast potatoes.

"It really makes me sad," she went on. "I could tell right away that Jack and his wife don't appreciate Aunt Betsy's highboy, the way they've shoved it into a corner behind the door to the patio." She helped herself to gravy. "Jack says it's because he can't get it to stand steady, and the drawers always stick."

"Well, perhaps they do," I said. "After all, the piece must be over two hundred years old."

But Buffy wouldn't agree. Aunt Betsy had never had that sort of trouble, she told me. If the highboy wobbled it was probably because the floors of Jack's contemporary house were subsiding; you couldn't trust architects these days.

It was true, her aunt had said that the highboy was temperamental. Usually the drawers would slide open as smoothly as butter, but now and then they seized up. It probably had something to do with the humidity, I thought; but according to Buffy her Aunt Betsy, who seems to have had the same sort of childish imagination as her niece, used to say that the highboy was sulking; someone had been rough with it, she would suggest, or it hadn't been polished lately.

"I'm sure Jack's wife doesn't know how to take care of good furniture properly either," Buffy went on after the salad had been served. "She's too busy with her high-powered executive job." Buffy had never worked a day in her life.

"Honestly, Janet, it's true," she said, mistaking my smile for skepticism. "When I was there last week the finish was already beginning to look dull, almost soapy. Aunt Betsy always used to polish it once a week with beeswax, to keep the patina. I mentioned that twice, but I could see Jack's wife wasn't paying any attention. Not that she ever pays any attention to me." Buffy gave a little nervous giggle, more of a hiccup really. Her brother's wife wasn't the only one of the family who thought of her as a lightweight, and she wasn't too silly to know it.

"What I suspect is, Janet, I suspect she's letting her cleaning lady spray it with that awful synthetic no-rub polish they make now," Buffy went on, frowning across the glazed damask. "I found a can of the stuff under her sink. Full of awful chemicals you can't pronounce. Anyhow, I'm sure the climate in Stonington can't be good for old furniture; not with all that nasty salt and damp in the air."

There was a lull in the conversation then, and at the other end of the table Buffy's husband heard her and gave a kind of guffaw. "Say, Clark," he called to my husband. "I wish you'd tell Buffy to forget about that dumb highboy of her aunt's."

Well, naturally Clark was not going to do anything of the sort. But he turned and listened patiently to Buffy's story, and then he suggested that she ask her brother if he'd be willing to exchange the highboy for her aunt's coffee service.

I THOUGHT THIS was a good idea, and so did Buffy. She wrote off to her brother, and the following Sunday evening, before she'd even expected an answer, Jack phoned to say that was fine by him. He was sick of the thing; no matter how he tried to prop up the legs it still wobbled.

Besides, the day before he'd gone to get out some maps for a trip they were planning, and the whole thing just kind of seized up. He'd stopped trying to free the top drawer with a screwdriver and was working on one of the lower ones, when he got a hell of a crack on the head. He must have loosened something somehow, he told Buffy, so that when he pulled on the lower drawer the upper one slid out noiselessly above him. And when he stood up, bingo.

It was Saturday, and their doctor was off call, so Jack's wife had to drive him ten miles to the Westerly emergency room; he was too dizzy and confused to drive himself. There wasn't any concussion, according to the X rays, but he had a lump on his head the size of a plum and a headache the size of a football. He'd be happy to ship that goddamned piece of furniture out of his house as soon as it was convenient, he told Buffy, and she could take her time about sending along the coffee service.

TWO WEEKS LATER when I went over to Buffy's for tea her aunt's highboy had arrived. She was so happy that I bore with her when she started being silly about how it appreciated the care she was taking of it. "When I rub in the beeswax I can almost feel it purring under my hand like a big cat," she insisted, giggling.

I glanced at the highboy again. I thought I'd never seen a less agreeable-looking piece of furniture. Its pretentious high-arched bonnet top resembled a clumsy mahogany Napoleon hat, and the ball-and-claw feet made the thing look as if it were up on tiptoe. If it was a big cat, it was a cat with bird's legs—a sort of gryphon.

"I know it's grateful to be here," Buffy told me. "The other day I couldn't find my reading glasses anywhere; but then, as I was standing in the sitting room, at my wit's end, I heard a little creak, or maybe it was more sort of a pop. I looked round and one of the top drawers of the highboy was out about an inch. Well, I went to shut it, and there were my glasses! Now what do you make of that?"

I made nothing of it, but humored her. "Quite a coincidence."

"Oh, more than that." Buffy gave another rippling giggle. "And it's completely steady now. Try and see."

I put a hand on one side of the highboy and gave the thing a little push, and she was perfectly right. It stood solid and heavy against the cream and yellow Colonial Williamsburg wallpaper, as if it had been in Buffy's house for centuries. The prune-dark mahogany was waxy to the touch, and colder than I would have expected.

"And the drawers don't stick in the least." Buffy slid them open and shut to demonstrate. "I know it's going to be happy here."

IT WAS EARLY SPRING when the highboy arrived, and whether or not it was happy, it gave no trouble until that summer. Then in July we had a week of drenching thunderstorms, and the drawers began to jam. I saw it happen one Sunday when Clark and I were over and Bobby tried to get out the slides of their recent trip to Quebec. He started shaking the thing and swore a bit, and Buffy had to go and help him.

"There's nothing at all wrong with the highboy," she whispered to me afterward. "Bobby just doesn't understand how to treat it. You mustn't force the drawers open like that; you have to be gentle."

After we'd sat through the slides, Bobby went over to the highboy again to put them away.

"Careful, darling," Buffy warned him.

"Okay, okay," Bobby said; but it was clear he wasn't listening seriously. He yanked the drawer open without much trouble; but when he slammed it shut he let out a frightful howl: he'd shut his right thumb inside.

"Christ, will you look at that!" he shouted, holding out his stubby red hand to show us a deep dented gash below the knuckle. "I think the damn thing's broken."

WELL, BOBBY'S THUMB wasn't broken; but it was bruised rather badly, as things turned out. His hand was swollen for over a week, so that he couldn't play in the golf tournament at the club, which meant a lot to him.

Buffy and I were sitting on the clubhouse terrace that day, and Bobby was moseying about by the first tee in a baby-blue golf shirt, with his hand still wadded up in bandages.

"Poor darling, he's so cross," Buffy said.

"Cross?" I asked; in fact Bobby didn't look cross, only foolish and disconsolate.

"He's furious at the highboy, you know, Janet," she said. "And what I've decided is, there's no point any longer in trying to persuade him to treat it right. After what happened last week, I realized it would be better to keep them apart. So I've simply moved all his things out of the drawers, and now I'm using them for my writing paper and tapestry wools."

This time, perhaps because it was such a sticky hot day and there were too many flies on the terrace, I felt more than usually impatient with Buffy's whimsy. "Really, dear, you mustn't let your imagination run away with you," I said, squeezing more lemon into my iced tea. "Your aunt's highboy doesn't have any quarrel with Bobby. It isn't a human being, it's a piece of furniture."

"But that's just it," Buffy insisted. "That's why it matters so much. I mean, you and I, and everybody else." She waved her plump little freckled hand at the other people under their pink and white umbrellas, and the golfers scattered over the rolling green plush of the course. "We all know we've got to die sooner or later, no matter how careful we are. Isn't that so?"

"Well, yes," I admitted.

"But furniture and things can be practically immortal, if they're lucky. A heirloom piece like Aunt Betsy's highboy— I really feel I've got an obligation to preserve it, you know."

"For the children and grandchildren, you mean."

"Oh, that too, certainly. But they're just temporary themselves, you know." Buffy took a gulp of the hot summer air. "You see, from our point of view we own our things. But really, as far as they're concerned we're only looking after them for a while. We're just caretakers, like poor old Billy here at the club." She giggled.

"He's retiring this year, I heard," I said, hoping to change the subject.

"Yes. But they'll hire someone else, you know, and if he's competent it won't make much difference to us. Well, it's the same with our things, Janet. Naturally they want to do whatever they can to preserve themselves, and to find the best possible caretakers. They don't ask much: just to be polished regularly, and not to have their drawers wrenched open and slammed shut. And of course they don't want to get cold or wet or dirty, or have lighted cigarettes put down on them, or drinks or houseplants."

"It sounds like quite a lot to ask," I said.

"But Janet, it's so important for them!" Buffy cried. "Of course it was naughty of the highboy to give Bobby such a bad pinch, but I think it was understandable. He was being awfully rough, and it got frightened."

"Now, Buffy," I said, stirring my iced tea so that the cubes clinked impatiently. "You can't possibly believe that we're all in danger of being injured by our possessions."

"Oh no," she said, with another little rippling giggle. "Most of them don't have the strength to do any serious damage. But I'm not worried anyhow. I have a lovely relationship with all my nice things: they know I have their best interests at heart."

I DIDN'T SCOLD Buffy anymore; it was too hot, and I realized there wasn't any point. My sister-in-law was fifty-six years old, and if she hadn't grown up by then, she probably never would. Anyhow, I heard no more about the highboy until about a month later, when Buffy's grandchildren were staying with her. One hazy damp afternoon in August I drove over to the house with a basket of surplus tomatoes and zucchini. The children were building with blocks, and Buffy was sitting near them working on a gros-point cushion-cover design from the Metropolitan Museum. After a while she needed more pink wool; so she asked her grandson, who was about six, to run over to the highboy and fetch it.

He got up and went at once—he's really a very nice little boy. But when he pulled on the bottom drawer it wouldn't come out, and he gave the bird leg a little kick. It was nothing serious, but Buffy screamed and leapt up as if she had been stung, spilling her canvas and colored wools.

"Jamie!" Really, she was almost shrieking. "You must never, never do that!" And she grabbed him by the arm and dragged him away roughly.

Well naturally the child was shocked and upset; he cast a

terrified look at Buffy and burst into tears. That brought her to her senses. She hugged him and explained that Grandma wasn't angry; but he must be very, very careful of the highboy, because it was so old and valuable.

I thought Buffy had overreacted terribly, and when she went out to the kitchen to fix gin and tonics, and milk and peanut butter cookies for the children, "to settle us all down," I followed her in and told her so. Surely, I said, she cared more for her grandchildren than she did for her furniture.

Buffy gave me an odd look; then she pushed the swing door shut.

"You don't understand, Janet," she said in a low voice, as if someone might hear. "Jamie really mustn't annoy the highboy. It's been rather difficult lately, you see." She tried to open a bottle of tonic, but couldn't—I had to take it from her.

"Oh, thank you," she said distractedly. "It's just— Well, for instance. The other day Mary Lee was playing house under the highboy: she'd made a kind of nest for herself with the sofa pillows, and she had some of her dolls in there. I don't know what happened exactly, but I think one of the claw feet gave her that nasty-looking scratch on her leg." Buffy looked over her shoulder apprehensively and spoke even lower. "And there've been other incidents— Oh, never mind." She sighed, then giggled. "I know you think it's all perfect nonsense, Janet. Would you like lime or lemon?"

I was disturbed by this conversation, and that evening I told Clark so; but he made light of it. "Darling, I wouldn't worry. It's just Buffy's usual sort of whimsy."

"Well, but this time she was carrying the joke too far," I said. "She really frightened those children. And even if she was partly fooling, I think she cares far too much about her old furniture. Really, it made me cross."

"I think you should feel sorry for Buffy," Clark remarked. "You know what we've said so often: now that she's had to give up sports, she doesn't have enough to do. I expect she's just trying to add a little interest to her life."

I said that perhaps he was right. And then I had an idea: I'd get Buffy elected secretary of the Historical Society, to fill out the term of the woman who'd just resigned. I knew it wouldn't be easy, because she had no experience and a lot of people thought she was a little flighty. But I was sure she could do it; she'd always run that big house perfectly, and she knew lots about local history and genealogy and antiques.

First I had to convince the Historical Society board that they wanted her, and then I had to convince Buffy; but I managed. I was quite proud of myself. And I was even prouder as time went on and she not only did the job beautifully, she seemed to have forgotten all that nonsense about the highboy. That whole fall and winter she didn't mention it even once.

It wasn't until early the following spring that Buffy phoned one morning, in what was obviously rather a state, and asked me to come over. I found her waiting in the front hall, wearing her white quilted parka. Her fine blonde-tinted curls were all over the place, her eyes unnaturally round and bright, and the tip of her snub nose pink; she looked like a distracted rabbit.

"Don't take off your coat yet, Janet," she told me almost breathlessly. "Come out into the garden; I must show you something."

I was surprised, because it was a cold blowy day in March. Apart from a few snowdrops and frozen-looking white crocus scattered over the lawn, there was nothing to see. But it wasn't the garden Buffy had on her mind.

"You know that woman from New York, that Abigail Jones, who spoke on 'Decorating with Antiques' yesterday at the Society?" she asked as we stood between two beds of spaded earth and sodden compost.

"Mm," I agreed.

"Well, I was talking to her after the lecture, and I invited her to come for brunch this morning and see the house."

"Mm? And how did that go?"

"It was awful, Janet. I don't mean—" Buffy hunched her shoulders against the damp wind and swallowed as if she were about to sob. "I mean, Mrs. Jones was very pleasant. She admired my Hepplewhite table and chairs; and she was very nice about the canopy bed in the blue room too, though I felt I had to tell her that one of the posts wasn't original. But what she liked best was Aunt Betsy's highboy."

"Oh yes?"

"She thought it was a really fine piece. I told her we'd always believed it was made in Newport, but Mrs. Jones thought Salem was more likely. Well, that naturally made me uneasy."

"What? I mean, why?"

"Because of the witches, you know." Buffy gave her nervous giggle. "Then she said she hoped I was taking good care of it. So of course I told her I was. Mrs. Jones said she could see that, but what I should realize was that my highboy was quite unique, with the carved feathering of the legs, and what looked like all the original hardware. It really ought to be in a museum, she said. I tried to stop her, because I could tell the highboy was getting upset."

"Upset?" I laughed, because I still assumed—or hoped—that it was a joke. "Why should it be upset? I should think it would be pleased to be admired by an expert."

"But don't you see, Janet?" Buffy almost wailed. "It didn't know about museums before. It didn't realize that there were places where it could be well taken care of and perfectly safe for, well, almost forever. It wouldn't know about them, you see, because when pieces of furniture go to a museum they don't come back to tell the others. It's like our going to heaven, I suppose. But now the highboy knows, that's what it will want."

"But a piece of furniture can't force you to send it to a museum," I protested, thinking how crazy this conversation would sound to anyone who didn't know Buffy.

"Oh, can't it." She brushed her wispy curls out of her face. "You don't know what it can do, Janet. None of us does. There've been things I didn't tell you about— But never mind that. Only in fairness I must say I'm beginning to have a different idea of why Aunt Betsy didn't leave the highboy to me in the first place. I don't think it was because of the Lumpkin name at all. I think she was trying to protect me." She giggled again, with a sound like ice cracking.

"Really, Buffy—" Wearily, warily, I played along. "If it's as clever as you say, the highboy must know Mrs. Jones was just being polite. She didn't really mean—"

"But she did, you see. She said that if I ever thought of donating the piece to a museum, where it could be really well cared for, she hoped I would let her know. I tried to change the subject, but I couldn't. She went on telling me how there was always the danger of fire or theft in a private home. She said home instead of house, that's the kind of woman she is." Buffy giggled again. "Then she started to talk about tax deductions, and said she knew of several places that would be interested. I didn't know what to do; I told her that if I did ever decide to part with the highboy I'd probably give it to our Historical Society."

"Well, of course you could," I suggested. "If you felt—"

"But it doesn't matter now," Buffy interrupted, putting a small cold plump hand on my wrist. "I was weak for a moment, but I'm not going to let it push me around. I've worked out what to do to protect myself: I'm changing my will. I called Toni Stevenson already, and I'm going straight over to her office after you leave."

"You're willing the highboy to the Historical Society?" I asked.

"Well, maybe eventually, if I have to. Not outright; heavens, no. That would be fatal. For the moment I'm going to leave it to Bobby's nephew Fred. But only in case of my accidental death." Behind her distracted wisps of hair, Buffy gave a very peculiar little smile.

"Death!" I swallowed. "You don't really think—"

"I think that highboy is capable of absolutely anything. It has no feelings, no gratitude at all. I suppose that's because from its point of view I'm going to die so soon anyway."

"But, Buffy—" The hard wind whisked away the rest of my words, but I doubt if she would have heard them.

"Anyhow, what I'd like you to do now, Janet, is come in with me and be a witness when I tell it what I've planned."

I was almost sure then that Buffy had gone a bit mad; but of course I went back indoors with her.

"Oh, I wanted to tell you, Janet," she said in an unnaturally loud, clear voice when we reached the sitting room. "Now that I know how valuable Aunt Betsy's highboy is, I've decided to leave it to the Historical Society. I put it in my will today. That's if I die of natural causes, of course. But if it's an accidental death, then I'm giving it to my husband's nephew, Fred Turner." She paused and took a loud breath.

"Really," I said, feeling as if I were in some sort of absurdist play.

"I realize the highboy may feel a little out of place in Fred's house," Buffy went on relentlessly, "because he and his wife have all that weird modern canvas and chrome furniture. But I don't really mind about that. And of course Fred's a little careless sometimes. Once when he was here he left a cigarette burning on the cherry pie table in the study; that's how it got that ugly scorch mark, you know. And he's rather thoughtless about wet glasses and coffee cups too." Though Buffy was still facing me, she kept glancing over my left shoulder toward the highboy.

I turned to follow her gaze, and suddenly for a moment I shared her delusion. The highboy had not moved; but now it looked heavy and sullen, and it seemed to have developed a kind of vestigial face. The brass pulls of the two top drawers formed the half-shut eyes of this face, and the fluted column between them was its long thin nose; the ornamental brass keyhole of the full-length drawer below supplied a pursed, tight mouth. Under its curved mahogany tricorn hat, it had a mean, calculating expression, like some hypocritical New England Colonial merchant.

"I know exactly what you're thinking," Buffy said, abandoning the pretense of speaking to me. "And if you don't behave yourself, I might give you to Fred and Roo right now. They have children too. Very active children, not nice quiet ones like Jamie and Mary Lee." Her giggle had a chilling fragmented sound now; ice shivering into shreds.

"NONE OF THAT was true about Bobby's nephew, you know," Buffy confided as she walked me to my car. "They're not really careless, and neither of them smokes. I just wanted to frighten it."

"You rather frightened me," I told her.

Which was no lie, as I said to Clark that evening. It wasn't just the strength of Buffy's delusion, but the way I'd been infected by it. He laughed and said he'd never known she could be so convincing. Also he asked if I was sure she hadn't been teasing me.

Well, I had to admit I wasn't. But I was still worried. Didn't he think we should do something?

"Do what?" Clark said. And he pointed out that even if Buffy hadn't been teasing, he didn't imagine I'd have much luck trying to get her to a therapist; she thought psychologists were completely bogus. He said we should just wait and see what happened.

All the same, the next time I saw Buffy I couldn't help inquiring about the highboy. "Oh, everything's fine now," she said, laughing lightly. "Right after I saw you I signed the codicil. I put a copy in one of the drawers to remind it, and it's been as good as gold ever since."

SEVERAL MONTHS PASSED, and Buffy never mentioned the subject again. When I finally asked how the highboy was, she said, "What? Oh, fine, thanks," in an uninterested way that suggested she'd forgotten her obsession—or tired of her joke.

The irritating thing was that now that I'd seen the unpleasant face of the highboy, it was there every time I went to the house. I would look from it to Buffy's round pink-nosed face, and wonder if she had been laughing at me all along.

Finally, though, I began to forget the whole thing. Then one day late that summer Clark's nephew's wife Roo was at our house. She's a photographer, quite a successful one, and she'd come to take a picture of me.

As many photographers do, Roo always kept up a more or less mindless conversation with her subjects as she worked; trying to prevent them from getting stiff and self-conscious, I suppose.

"I like your house, you know, Janet," she said. "You have such simple, great-looking things. Could you turn slowly to the right a little? . . . Good. Hold it. . . . Now over at Uncle Bobby's—Hold it. . . . The garden's great of course, but I don't care much for their furniture. Lower your chin a little, please . . . You know that big dark old chest of drawers, that Buffy's left to Fred."

"The highboy," I said.

"Right. Let's move those roses over a little. That's better. . . . It's supposed to be so valuable, but I think it's hideous. I told Fred I didn't want it around. Hold it. Okay."

"And what did he say?" I asked.

"Huh? Oh, he feels the same as I do. He said that if he did inherit the thing he was going to give it to a museum."

"A museum?" I have to admit that my voice rose. "Where was Fred when he told you this?"

"Don't move, please. Okay. . . . What? I think we were in Buffy's sitting room; but she wasn't there, of course. You don't have to worry, Janet. Fred wouldn't say anything like that in front of his aunt; he knows it would sound awfully ungrateful."

Well, my first impulse was to pick up the phone and warn my sister-in-law as soon as Roo left. But then I thought that would sound ridiculous. It was crazy to imagine that Buffy was in danger from a chest of drawers. Especially long after she'd gotten over the idea herself, if she'd ever really had it in the first place.

Buffy might even laugh at me, I thought; she wasn't anywhere near as whimsical as she had been. She'd become more and more involved in the Historical Society, and it looked as if she'd be reelected automatically next year. Besides, if by chance she hadn't been kidding, and I reminded her of her old delusion and seemed to share it, the delusion might come back and it would be my fault.

So I didn't do anything. I didn't even mention the incident to Clark.

TWO DAYS LATER, while I was writing letters in the study, Clark burst in. I knew something awful had happened as soon as I saw his face.

Bobby had just called from the hospital, he told me. Buffy was in intensive care, and the prognosis was bad. She had a broken hip and a concussion, but the real problem was the shock to her weak heart. Apparently, he said, some big piece of furniture had fallen on her when she tried to pull open a drawer.

I didn't wait to ask what piece of furniture that was. I drove straight to the hospital with him: but by the time we got there Buffy was in a coma.

Though she was nearer plump than slim, she seemed horribly small in that room, on that high flat bed—like a kind of faded child. Her head was in bandages, and there were tubes and wires all over her like mechanical snakes; her little freckled hands lay in weak fists on the white hospital sheet. You could see right away that it was all over with her, though in fact they managed to keep her alive, if you can use that word, for nearly three days more.

FRED TURNER, just as he had promised, gave the highboy to a New York museum. I went to see it there recently. Behind its maroon velvet rope it looked exactly the same: tall, glossy, top-heavy, bird-legged and claw-footed.

"You wicked, selfish, ungrateful thing," I told it. "I hope you get termites. I hope some madman comes in here and attacks you with an axe."

The highboy did not answer me, of course. But under its mahogany Napoleon hat, it seemed to wear a little self-satisfied smile.

Counting
Sheep

THOUGH SHE TRIED not to show it, Janey Francis was surprised as well as pleased when she was asked to head the Wordsworth Project in Grasmere for the following year. As the only woman on the board she had always felt a little out of things. For most of her colleagues, as for Wordsworth himself, woman's role was to be intelligently supportive. Even now she suspected that some of them had doubts—not about her scholarship, but about her ability to run the program with sufficient detachment. From the start she had been typed—and teased—as maternally oversolicitous of their graduate fellows: "a nervous foster mum" as one put it.

What her colleagues didn't see, or wouldn't admit, was that living and working at Grasmere for an entire year wasn't easy for a young person. In fact, if one was not feeling at the top of one's form the Lake District wasn't the best place for anyone. Of course it was scenic, and wonderfully rich in associations, but if you didn't enjoy exploring the countryside you could be rather at a loss after working hours. And the truth is, many scholars love romantic nature in literature, but become quite helpless and bored outdoors.

Then, Cumbria is an odd part of England: still extremely backward and isolated in certain places, and full of legends and superstitions that were old in Wordsworth's time, some of them rather unpleasant. In bad weather there was an oppressive look about it: the fir-blackened glens like dark rents in the landscape, the steep stony sheep-littered hills. Besides, it really rained far too much, in Janey's opinion, and could be damp and chilly even in midsummer.

The new graduate fellows, arriving in late August, often came down with nasty colds. Most of them—you might even say the best of them—adjusted and survived, even prospered. But occasionally, especially if they were used to warmer climates, or missed their Significant Others, they became nervous and miserable. Last year a young American woman had walked out of the Project after only a month mainly because, so she claimed, her underthings took three days to dry. As Jim Stephens, who was running things this year, put it, the weather in Grasmere definitely separated the sheep from the goats.

Janey had been concerned about Robbie McEwen almost from the day he was hired, though she didn't mention it at first. He was a serious young man with a long pale face and thick curly colorless hair and a blurred, distracted manner. He was certainly odd, but one had to expect textual scholars to be a bit odd. A life devoted to someone else's words —to following along behind earlier readers, checking their work, correcting their errors and biases—it wasn't easy, as she well knew. One thing that made it especially hard was the daily, hourly attempt to rule out everything personal that might influence an editorial decision—that had to make you a little unreal and abstracted.

You had to have a personal life, just for balance. You had to have friends and family, and in Robbie's case there didn't seem to be any. He was an only child and—odd, in this day—an orphan, and even his most favorable letters of recommendation had given the impression that the writers didn't know him very well.

Then, on top of that, there was the natural anxiety and depression so many young British academics suffered from these days as a result of government cuts in education. Usually they had almost no chance of a decent job unless they'd got connections. Robbie's current situation wasn't promising. He had an only moderately good degree from London University, and was living at Grasmere and working as a junior editor on one of the later volumes—a fairly unimportant one—and helping out as a tour guide at Dove Cottage. If he could come up with a couple of interesting articles or a book he might find an appointment somewhere, but it was rather a long shot.

WHEN JANEY ARRIVED for the fall meeting of the board, Robbie seemed to have settled in fairly well, though Jim Stephens said he didn't spend much time with the other fellows. Now and then Robbie would go with them to the pub, but more often he'd be out hiking in the woods or up on the fells, even in the worst weather. Though he was a scholarship boy from North London and had never lived in the country before, he'd become very keen. In only two months he'd made himself remarkably knowledgeable: he knew the good trails, and where to avoid bogs and rock slides; he could tell gorse from broom and a flycatcher from a finch at twenty yards. Janey wasn't too surprised; she remembered Robbie declaring at his interview that Wordsworth's search for unity with the natural world was what had first drawn him to the poet.

He'd turned out to be quite a good editor too. Jim Stephens said he'd already found some passages in an obscure letter to Wordsworth that seemed to be echoed in the poems. The problem was that one of the other graduate fellows was trumpeting the discovery about as if it were his own. Janey didn't like the sound of that, and volunteered to speak to Robbie about it.

She found him upstairs in the library: a big shadowy room full of reference books and manuscript boxes and the sort of computers and copy machines that always reminded her of microwave ovens. Whether they processed food or words, Janey didn't care for them; she was pleased to see Robbie writing with a pencil at one of the long oak tables.

When she said she'd come to have a look at the letter he'd discovered, he jumped up eagerly and brought out a heavy transparent envelope.

"If you'll look on page three, that's where he uses the phrase: 'I believe that the same spirit moves all created beings and all the objects of their thought.' Almost exactly what Wordsworth wrote in *Tintern*." Like most people on the Project, Robbie referred to the major works by nicknames: Fits, Leeches, Reaper, Seven, and so on. Yet his tone was reverent, and he held the plastic envelope as a minor priest might hold the reliquary of a minor saint.

Carefully, Janey slid out the yellow, flaking sheets and peered at the loopy tangled handwriting, blurred by time to tobacco brown. She knew it was the words that counted in literary history, not the bits of paper or parchment on which they were first incised; still, she could never help being moved by a holograph. Wordsworth himself had held this letter, broken its seal (the darkened waxy stain was still visible), read the lines she was reading now—

"Yes. Yes, I see," she murmured. Then she shook herself awake, returned the letter to its case, and set about her task. "Jim Stephens tells me it was you who found this passage, not anyone else," she told Robbie. "I hope you're going to write it up as soon as possible, so you can get credit."

"I d'know," he replied vaguely, running his hand through colorless matted curls. "I think Horace Blow has already started something, actually."

"Well, then you'd better tell him to stop," said Janey. "This is your discovery, not his." She shook the plastic envelope at Robbie, but all she got was a look of curatorial anxiety as the pages inside slid back and forth.

"I d'know," he mumbled. "I mean I told Horace, if he wants to— I mean, it won't make any difference to the Project who writes the article, will it?"

"No, but it could make a difference to you," Janey said a little sharply. In this profession, as she knew quite well, you really had to blow your own horn a little, and Robbie didn't even seem to own such an instrument. "To your career."

"Oh, I don't care about that," he said.

Janey sighed. Apparently, Robbie had cast himself in the role of one of Wordsworth's humble, all-accepting peasants. But what might be appropriate behavior for an elderly Leech-Gatherer was ridiculous in a young man in need of academic employment. "Well, you should," she scolded.

Robbie did not answer, only gazed past her, his dark, slightly protuberant eyes fixed on the middle distance. Janey glanced round, but saw no one. "Think about it, at least," she said, handing the letter back.

"Um, sure," he replied, in a tone she recognized from raising four children as the Yes that means No.

Janey left the library feeling cross. She realized that either Jim Stephens or she, perhaps both of them, would now have to speak to the presumptuous Horace. Robbie was not going to fight for his discovery, or complain if it were taken away from him, any more than he had complained earlier about his dismal accommodations. He had been assigned two dank little rooms in a hillside cottage on the other side of the lake, backed up to a cold, noisy stream. There was electricity but no gas, and the sanitary facilities were out-doors. Jim used to excuse such places to the fellows by claiming that they would provide a historically authentic experience. Wordsworth and his sister Dorothy lived that way or worse in Dove Cottage, he'd say. Which was proba-bly true, she thought; indeed Dorothy might have been grateful for Robbie's electric light and hot plate and one-bar heater.

THOUGH JANEY was irritated by this episode, she didn't become really worried about Robbie until after the spring meeting of the board. At that time the Project director al-ways tried to have an informal talk with each of the fellows to discuss their future prospects and if necessary organize letters and recommendations. Janey was involved because it was now definitely arranged that she would take a leave from her university and run the Project the following year. She was looking forward to it—the relief from committee meetings and college politics, the experience of being in Grasmere for twelve months. There was a kind of genius of place, after all, that could make a difference to a scholar.

Janey hadn't been able to find Robbie in the pub—Jim said he seldom went there anymore—so she stopped him one afternoon as he was finishing his shift at Dove Cottage. She asked if he was planning a hike, and suggested that he walk round Grasmere with her. She could tell it wasn't what he'd had in mind, but he agreed.

It was a cool, hazy day in late May. There'd been a spell of heavy sopping-wet weather, and the landscape was densely mossy and green. As they left the road and went down toward the lake through the woods there were flow-ers everywhere, varnished-yellow buttercups and pale-blue lace drifts of forget-me-nots, and unseen birds chirping and trilling.

Janey had already caught up on how Robbie's volume of the Works and his article were coming along—the former well enough; the latter—in spite of both Jim's and her efforts—now under the co-authorship of Horace Blow. When they stopped by the shore she asked about Robbie's plans for the fall. He should have expected this; but he gave a kind of gulp and said he hadn't really thought about it.

"Well," said she, trying to strike a tone between jovial and serious, "you'd better start thinking."

It was as if Robbie hadn't heard her.

"Look," he said, gazing at the pale shimmering mirror of the lake and the floating gauzy clouds reflected there, silver-blue and silver-grey.

"Yes, very nice," Janey said, willing to indulge him for the moment. It was quite natural for the graduate fellows—and often the more senior people too—to form a romantic attachment to some transcendental Wordsworthian subject. For her, years ago, it had been the yew tree in Lorton Vale. Usually these enthusiasms were harmless—a particular path over the fells mentioned in the journals, the spring flood of daffodils in the woods by Grasmere. A couple of times, though, someone had confused art and life, and became overinvolved with a local girl as simpleminded and plain as Janey had always suspected Wordsworth's Lucy to have been.

She held her peace for a count of twenty; then resumed, "As I was saying, you should consider—"

Robbie didn't answer; he merely turned rudely and started walking on along the slaty shore, setting a brisk pace.

"Really," she called, almost running to catch up with him, putting one foot in a puddle in the process. "You've damn well got to think about it. Your fellowship ends in

August; you should be planning your future now, while we can help you."

Robbie paused and looked at her over the shoulder of his fuzzy duffel coat with a suspicious adversary expression. "What I want is to stay here," he announced.

"I'm sorry, but that's completely out of the question," Janey said. It wasn't completely out of the question, she realized even as she spoke: there was that young man from Kansas three years ago—

"I can't imagine leaving Grasmere," Robbie declared, as if to himself. "I belong here." He gave a little shake of the head and walked on.

"I do understand that feeling, especially on a beautiful day like this," Janey cried, scrambling after him through the yellow-green fringes of a willow and trying to keep her temper. "But you have to grow up and face facts."

Robbie must have heard, but he didn't reply or look back; only strode on as if he were alone. Janey plodded after him, one foot squelching cold, muddy water. Maybe he could stay on, she said to herself; you could ask Jim Stephens. But she could already see the patronizing smile that would appear on Jim's face. "Well of course he wants to stay on, it beats finding a job," he would say. And if she persisted, pleading Robbie's case, Jim would give her a look that announced as clear as day, You are a weak, susceptible woman.

Besides, she didn't owe Robbie anything, Janey thought as they tramped on silently in single file. She was panting now, trying to keep up; one cheek stung where he had let a branch whip back into it, and her shoe was full of cold mud. He was a thoughtless, inconsiderate young man, and if he stayed on next year she'd have to cope with him on a daily basis.

The lakeside path ended. Panting, fuming, Janey climbed the steep grassy slope to where Robbie was waiting by the stile. She paused a moment to recover her breath and her equanimity, then passed through onto the byroad that led to his cottage. Furious though she was, she recognized the charm of the scene. The narrow road was edged by loose green waves of weeds foaming at their crests into white cow parsley, and down by the bend an escaped sheep was browsing.

Janey wasn't surprised to see it. Though sheep are part of the landscape in the Lake District, they are also a public nuisance. They break through hedgerows and wander into gardens—including the garden of Dove Cottage—and destroy flowers and vegetables; and they are always getting tangled in fences and stumbling into sinkholes.

When Robbie followed Janey through the stile he saw the same thing. He swore to himself quietly; then he shouted, "Out again!" and started running toward the sheep.

"Bad girl!" he scolded as he came nearer. "Baa!" He swerved and made a rush at the animal, waving both arms and shooing it toward a half-open gate. It trotted forward with the slightly comic and mechanical motion all sheep have, then balked and wobbled sideways. "Oh no, love, you don't want to do that," he cried, heading the creature in with a shove and a pat.

"Right," he said finally, latching the gate and leaning on it, gazing up the steep field, where three or four other sheep with the same red dye mark on their woolly haunches were grazing among clumps of spiky, gold-flowering gorse.

"Wonderful, aren't they?" he asked.

Janey didn't answer. She was still cross and out of breath, and besides she didn't agree. Though they might look picturesque at a distance, she found sheep unattractive up close. For one thing, they were dirty—those fluffy white rugs in the local shops were the result of a long clean-up effort. Wool on the hoof was a mass of long grimy albino dreadlocks, matted with straw and burrs and caked at the wrong end with dried excrement. Whenever you tried to go for a walk or a picnic in the Lake District, the sheep had always got there first. Anywhere you might want to sit down, the turf had been churned by their muddy hooves and littered with their droppings, like greasy brown bunches of grapes.

"Really, they ought to be able to keep those silly animals off the road," she complained as Robbie's sheep waddled upward to join the others.

"Not this one," said Robbie, chewing meditatively on a stem of grass as he watched. "She's always in trouble. Very naughty, aren't you?" he called. "Baa!"

It was quite a good imitation, and not only his sheep but one or two others raised their heads and replied: "Baa!"

"You know that particular animal?" Janey asked.

"Rather."

"Oh—is she the one you rescued last winter?"

"That's her."

Janey knew the story; everyone did. Late one freezing February evening when Robbie was on his way home from the Project library he heard a sheep bleating miserably. Most people would have walked on, but he climbed down off the road and found a young ewe stuck in the broken ice and mud of a drainage ditch. He couldn't budge the animal himself, so he ran to the nearest farm and told the farmer and together they pulled her out and carried her home.

The Project got a lot of credit locally for this good deed, and so did Robbie. As Jim Stephens had pointed out at the time, there was even a precedent, in Wordsworth's "The Idle Shepherds," where a sheep caught in a ravine is rescued by a Poet. The Project didn't have a Poet on hand, but all the same Robbie was keeping up the tradition. It was probably natural for him to take an interest in the animal's welfare after that, Janey thought.

————

THE NEXT AFTERNOON Janey went over the list of fellows with Jim. He'd talked to Robbie too, and suggested some secondary-school jobs he might apply for, and a program that sent teachers to Africa. Jim's opinion was that between them they'd done enough.

Janey agreed, but privately she wondered if she could have been more persistent, or more tactful. Probably that was why, a few days later, she invited Robbie to join her and two American acquaintances, Julian and Mary Ann Fenn, who were visiting the Lake District for the first time. They'd rented a car and wanted to drive up toward Derwentwater and Buttermere. The invitation would show Robbie that she was still concerned about him, she thought; and his local expertise might be interesting to the Fenns.

They had unsettled weather for the drive: windy, with heavy, low-scudding clouds. And Robbie was in an unsettled mood himself, alternatively voluble and silent. Though he pointed out landmarks, and discoursed interestingly on local history and geology, his manner made Janey uneasy. It seemed not only depressed but competitive—not so much with her as with Wordsworth. Two or three times Robbie remarked that the poet hadn't ever been up a certain valley, or had mistaken the name of some bird or bush. And quite often, when Julian or Mary Ann asked a question, he seemed not to have heard.

Still, everything went fairly smoothly except for one moment up in Honister Pass, when Mary Ann said how sad and boring it must be to be a stupid sheep, with nothing to do all day but chew grass and wait to be turned into lamb chops or shaved naked like a convict.

Robbie leant forward over the back of the seat. "That's a very ignorant remark," he declared. "These mountain sheep aren't stupid, they're quite intelligent really. They can survive for days under eight or ten feet of snow. And they have a very good life. They aren't killed for meat, and they don't dislike being sheared; they appreciate it, especially in hot weather. You'd understand if you'd ever watched," he went on less aggressively. "They don't struggle and kick: they fall into a kind of trance." He wouldn't mind being a sheep himself, he added, perhaps realizing he'd been rude and wanting to make a joke.

"Well, I guess it'd have some advantages," Julian said. "No responsibility for the way the world's going to hell, and you'd have your choice of the ewes."

Everyone laughed at that except Robbie. Janey could understand that: one of the greatest drawbacks of the Project for the male fellows was the shortage of female companionship. For some reason Wordsworth wasn't popular with young women scholars: there were never more than two or three in any year. As a result, every fall there was a mating flurry in which the less determined young men, like Robbie, always seemed to miss out.

The Fenns must have noticed his silence, but it all passed off. They had an agreeable tea in Keswick, though Robbie didn't say much, and didn't even answer when Julian asked what his plans were for next year.

After that they drove back by another route so the Fenns could see Castlerigg Stone Circle. Though this monument is said to have been built by the Druids, it's not much to look at: just a ring of lumpy grey stones standing in a rough-mown field. But it is dramatically placed: in a natural amphitheater of flat open countryside with impressive peaks round about.

Julian Fenn parked on the road by the gate, and they climbed the low rise to the stones. These seemed taller than Janey had remembered, and the rapid sweep of sun and shadow over the valley gave them an odd look—as if they were moving, wading in the tall coarse grass.

There were three or four other tourists wandering about, and some scruffy-looking people, hikers or hippies, camped just outside the circle of stones. One of them, a lanky young man with a blonde pigtail, was sitting cross-legged behind the largest fallen stone, with his eyes shut.

"What's he doing?" Mary Ann asked.

"Meditating, I suppose," Janey said. She took a step nearer to the rock. It was roughly oblong and patterned with the pale-red and pale-gold overlapping miniature flowers of lichen; in a kind of shallow depression on top there was a little heap of costume jewelry and a few coins.

"That's the wish stone," said a voice behind them. It was another hippie, a plump untidy young woman in a long draggled gypsy skirt.

"A wish stone, really?" Mary Ann turned. "How does it work?"

"Easy. All you do is, see, you place something of value on the stone, and make your wish."

"I've never heard of that custom," Janey said skeptically. "Have you, Robbie?"

He shook his head.

"Well, I'm going to make a wish anyhow," Mary Ann declared. She began to rummage in her tapestry handbag.

"Come on, honey." Julian lowered his voice. "You don't want to do that."

"Why not?" Mary Ann held up a fifty-pence piece. "I'll wish for good weather for the rest of our stay in the Lake District."

"Because it's a con, darling. It's not a folk tradition, or Robbie would have heard of it. And even if it were, you don't imagine some great hand's going to reach down from the sky and collect your fifty pence. That guy's just going to buy a pint with it."

"I don't care," Mary Ann said. "It's a nice idea." She scuffed across the field and dropped her coin, which rang loud in the silence. The meditating hippie did not move.

As Mary Ann returned, Julian started to speak again, but

he was distracted—they all were—by Robbie, who was now striding through the rough grass toward the wish stone with something clutched in one hand. When he placed this in the hollow, Janey could see it was his digital watch. Not an expensive one, but in terms of what the Project paid him, a considerable investment.

He stood there a moment, then started back. Behind and around him the pale grey rocks still seemed to be moving slightly as darker grey shadows of clouds flickered over them. Shadows slid over Robbie too, distorting his face and clothes so that for a moment he looked bunched up, misshapen. Janey had the idea that something was wrong; that what he'd just done was wrong, even dangerous. She opened her mouth to protest, then told herself not to be silly and shut it. If Robbie wanted to wish—no doubt for a job for next year—it was none of her affair.

THE NEXT MORNING the Fenns took off for Carlisle and the coast; they would return through Grasmere three days later and give Janey a lift to London. Those were three days of the best weather she'd ever known in the Lake District, but no one paid it much attention. The whole Project was in an uproar: Robbie McEwen had disappeared.

After the fact Janey remembered that he'd seemed especially preoccupied and withdrawn on the way back to Grasmere, and it turned out that nobody'd seen him again after they dropped him off at his cottage. There were police out searching, and nearly every amateur climber in the area, and eventually even a helicopter buzzing over the fells.

What everyone assumed was that Robbie had gone for a walk after supper, as he did most evenings. Then he'd had an accident: lost his footing on the loose stones of a scree, perhaps, or stepped into a rabbit hole and broken his leg.

That's what most people thought. Janey had another idea she didn't mention, but which preyed on her mind to an awful extent. She thought that maybe Robbie had decided to go off somewhere and kill himself, so he wouldn't have to leave Grasmere. She told herself that if so it would have been more rational to wait until August, but suicides aren't rational. That would explain why he hadn't been found: he knew the countryside well enough to choose some bog or ravine that would conceal a body permanently. She had trouble sleeping; she kept seeing Robbie drowned and swollen in the mud and weeds of some tarn, or crumpled in a dark crevice among broken stones.

Janey tried to argue herself out of these visions, but all the same she was relieved when the Fenns returned to Grasmere and Julian suggested another explanation: that Robbie McEwen had "done a bunk," as he put it.

She said she thought that wasn't likely, because Robbie had left everything he owned behind, including his clothes, wallet, and bank account. Not that there was much in the account: indeed, as it had turned out, he had an overdraft of nearly a thousand pounds.

"Well, that just about proves it," Julian said. "Sure he left his stuff; he wanted you to think he was dead. Then he probably just walked over the fells to some village twenty miles off where he's already got a nice new bank balance in another name."

"I don't think that's what happened," said Mary Ann. "I believe Robbie's still here, only we can't recognize him. You remember that afternoon at the Stone Circle? Well, what I think is, he wished he could stay in Grasmere, like you told us he wanted to; and so the wish stone turned him into a sheep."

"Darling," Julian protested.

"He said he'd like to be a sheep, I remember that," Mary Ann insisted, beginning to giggle. "And the wish stone worked for me, you know. We've had the most perfect weather." She waved at the sky, which had been a cloudless azure all day and was now darkening into cloudless indigo. "I'm positive that's what's happened to him."

THEY ALL LAUGHED THEN, and went on to other subjects, but somehow Mary Ann's silly idea stuck in Janey's mind. That night, in the confused and credulous state one sometimes slides into during insomnia, she remembered something the graduate fellow who'd left so abruptly the year before had said. She'd announced that the place was overrun with professors and sheep, and it was getting so you couldn't tell the professors from the sheep.

Janey thought how Wordsworth himself had been compared, in old age, to an old sheep—and somehow in the middle of the night it all seemed to hang together. She thought she even knew where Robbie would be now, if he were a sheep.

She knew those ideas were ridiculous, but she couldn't get them out of her head, or doze off. She unwound herself from a wrinkled sludge of blankets and sheets and took a sleeping pill, but it only made her dizzy and confused. Then she tried counting sheep, and that was worse, because they all had the faces of Wordsworth and his family, or people in the Project; and then one of them had her own face.

As soon as it began to get light Janey dragged on her clothes and went out. She took the direct route through the village, and when she reached the gate Robbie had shut she stopped and looked up the hillside through the cold grey mist, and it seemed to her that there were more sheep in the field than there'd been last time. But of course that didn't prove anything.

She leant on the splintery, weathered top rail and called out, "Baa!" Her imitation was far less convincing than Robbie's, and the sheep didn't answer or even look up.

"Baa!" she tried again. "Baaa!"

Most of the animals continued to munch grass with their

characteristic sideways tearing motion; but a young ram a little farther up the slope turned his head and stared at Janey over his matted fuzzy shoulder, in a fixed way she'd never seen a sheep do before.

"Baa!" he called shortly.

Janey stared back, wondering what he was doing there: normally the rams and ewes were separated until mating time in November. He looked exactly like the other sheep: dense yellowish-drab wool, incurled grey corrugated horns, long pale narrow face, and licorice eyes; but there was no red dye mark on his rump.

"All right. It's me," she imagined him bleating. "What are you going to do about it?"

THAT'S THE END of this story, except that Robbie McEwen was never found, alive or dead; and that sometime that morning, as Janey was packing, she decided she didn't want to run the Wordsworth Project the following year, or ever. Also it might be mentioned that later that same day, just as she and the Fenns drove out of Cumbria into Yorkshire, Mary Ann's spell of fine weather broke, and for the next month there was nothing but cold rain and fog and woolly drizzle all over northern England.

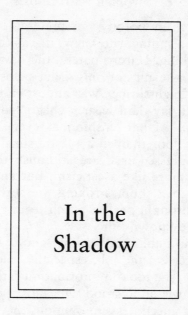

In the
Shadow

CELIA ZIMMERN was about the last person she, or
anyone else, would have expected to see a ghost. To the
other women who worked at the American Embassy in
London that year, she seemed almost unnaturally cool and
rational. Nothing ever rattled her, or—as far as they could
observe—deeply excited her.

Celia didn't even seem excited by her undoubted effect
on men—which she should have been, they thought, because there was really no explanation for it. She wasn't
beautiful, only rather pretty: slight, small, with a halo of
crinkly dark-oak hair and oak-brown eyes with lashes so
long and dense that some thought them false. Her manner
wasn't flirtatious or seductive, and she always dressed quietly. Most people didn't realize that Celia's fawn wool suit
was a thrift-shop Chanel, and her navy crepe a Jean Muir;
they only noticed that she wore the same clothes over and
over again.

For Celia, such monotony was preferable to its alternative. If she had a failing, she knew, it was that she wanted the best or nothing. Unfortunately, the best is usually expensive, and as a result not only Celia's closet but her tiny elegant flat in Knightsbridge was almost empty. She would rather shiver all day than wear a cheap synthetic sweater, rather sit on an Afghan cushion or even her beautifully waxed parquet floor than in a plastic sling chair. Her acquisitiveness expressed itself so fastidiously that most of the time it seemed more like asceticism. But anyone who had watched Celia in a shop, stroking the surface of a beige suede skirt or lifting a perfect peach from green tissue paper, would have known otherwise.

Celia made no public show of her good taste—or of any other preference. On the job, especially, she maintained a very low profile; she took in information rather than giving it out. She'd never understood why most people strove to repeat facts and anecdotes and opinions they already knew. Whereas by listening carefully one might hear something interesting, even something that would turn out to be useful.

Because Celia's manner was so low-key, members of the public tended to assume that she was employed at the embassy in some low-grade clerical capacity. In fact she was a career diplomat with a responsible position in the Information Section. Her attitude at work was one of polite attention to the matter at hand; but underneath this was an almost formidable administrative intelligence and decisiveness.

Though a few of Celia's female colleagues considered her somewhat poor in spirit as well as in wardrobe, most liked and even admired her. From their point of view her only fault was that she attracted too many men, and that she continued to go out with ones in whom she had no serious interest, constantly accompanying them to restaurants, concerts, theaters, and films. She was nearly thirty, they said to each other; why couldn't she settle on one guy and give somebody else a chance? It wasn't fair. "I don't even believe she sleeps with most of them," one irritable young woman from the Visa Office asserted, calling Celia "a bitch in the manger."

Celia herself was modest and a little cynical about her social success. She knew it was mostly her gift as a listener that attracted and held men, just as it soothed irritated officials and calmed impatient journalists. Somehow, she had the ability to focus her entire attention on whomever she was with, letting them speak at length without intruding any personal opinions. "That's very interesting," she would say if the monologue faltered. "Tell me more," or "Really! I never knew that."

What still rather surprised her was that none of the men she knew ever caught on. They took her ready responsiveness for granted, as they would that of a superior computer system. Indeed, she sometimes privately compared herself to those computer programs that can imitate psychotherapy and even produce a transference. A similar transference usually appeared in any man Celia went out with more than once or twice: a feeling of love and trust, and the conviction that she was deeply sympathetic with all his views. So strong was this conviction that often, even when Celia declined to put out, they wanted to continue seeing her, to engross her attention for life.

Celia was aware that her acquaintances wished she would settle on one guy, and also that she was twenty-nine. Even from the point of her career, marriage would be advisable. In this connection, her mind turned most often to an economist named Dwayne Mudd. He was a large handsome young man among whose many assets were good manners, sexual energy, professional competence, and a declared wish to have children. When she admitted to her friends that Dwayne was talking of marriage, they told her she could hardly do better. He was perfect, they said.

It was true, Celia admitted to herself, that Dwayne Mudd was a Rhodes scholar, a member of a well-known Midwestern political family, a former college track star, a *magna cum laude* graduate of Dartmouth, and an alumnus of Yale Law School, with what was probably a brilliant career ahead of him. Why was it, then, that when she imagined being married to him her strongest feeling was one of restless depression? Was it just his ridiculous name?

Or did it have something to do with the fact that Dwayne seemed to assume Celia was fortunate to be courted by him? When he told her that she was really very pretty, or that she would make an ideal diplomat's or politician's wife, she somehow felt he was giving himself a pep talk. He was excusing himself for not having chosen someone richer and more beautiful; above all, someone from another prominent Midwestern family, because as he had once remarked, in politics it's a big advantage to have a wife with good connections.

When Celia told Dwayne that she didn't think she would ever want to marry him, he didn't seem to hear her. "You can't mean that seriously, darling," he said. Even though she repeated it, he insisted on treating her reluctance as feminine coquettishness. "You'll come round," he said, smiling. "I can wait."

But Celia, though she told herself that she could hardly do better, was more and more determined not to come round. Privately, she had begun to refer to Dwayne as the Wombat; not only because of his admiration for Australia, where he had spent his last posting, but because of his cropped furry hair, broad and somewhat furry hands, solid build, and stubborn tenacity.

Usually Celia kept her growing annoyance with Dwayne to herself, but occasionally it slipped out. Once, for instance, he called her office four times in a single day, mainly to say that he was thinking of her and of what he referred to as "last night."

"He must love you very much," said her boss's secretary, Crystal, who was softly pretty and romantically inclined.

"Dwayne Mudd is a sentimentalist," replied Celia. "He probably read somewhere that women like this sort of constant nuisance and interruption."

A few days later, a cornucopia of sugar-pink rosebuds appeared on her desk at lunchtime.

"Oh, how lovely!" Crystal exclaimed.

"Well. Maybe," Celia said. "What I think is, if you're going to buy flowers, you should go to a flower shop. Anything you find on those stalls outside the underground is going to be dead before you get it home." She held the crumpled paper cone out horizontally, so that the weak stems, studded with knots of crumpled, rusting pink silk, drooped downward.

"But it's the thought that counts, isn't it?" Crystal asked.

Celia, who disagreed, did not contradict her. "You know what they always remind me of, flowers like these? Those shoddy cut-price umbrellas they sell in the same place, outside the Bond Street station. They never open right either, and quite soon they collapse completely."

"They're kind of sweet now, though, you know."

Crystal looked at the roses in a way that caused Celia to ask, "Would you like them?"

"Oh, yes! Thank you." Crystal raised the paper cornucopia to her lace-trimmed blouse and buried her nose in the faint fragrance.

"I guess Dwayne still wants to marry you," she said finally, exhaling.

"Yes." Celia gave a little apologetic laugh. "Of course that's impossible. I couldn't marry a man whose name was

Dwayne Mudd. Imagine what it would mean—a lifetime of bad jokes."

"You could keep your own last name. Lots of girls do that now," Crystal suggested.

"You'd still be married to him, and have to hear the jokes," said Celia. "Just for instance, Dwayne told me once that in elementary school he was known as 'Muddy Drain.'"

Crystal giggled. "But he must believe he still has a chance," she said. "After all, you keep seeing him. And you still have his mother's gold watch."

"Yes," Celia admitted. She lifted her slim hand, admiring again an exquisite bracelet watch made in the nineteen thirties by Cartier, with a woven gold mesh band and a tiny oblong dial elegantly engraved with Roman numerals. "But it's only a loan, you know. I've promised to return it the moment Dwayne finds someone else to marry."

"He'll never find anyone as long as you go on encouraging him," Crystal predicted.

"I don't encourage him," Celia protested mildly.

"You must, or he wouldn't still be hanging around. He'd find another girlfriend. I think really maybe you should give back his watch, and tell him you don't want to see him anymore." Crystal's voice shook slightly.

"But I do want to see Dwayne," Celia said, smiling, not offended—indeed, Crystal had never seen her offended. "He's quite pleasant to be with, and he knows a great deal about international economics and the Common Market. I just don't want to marry him. He realizes that."

"I don't think he does," said Crystal, who already had the difficult last name of Freeplatzer and felt she could reconcile herself to a lifetime of bad jokes quite easily if it should become Mudd. "But I suppose he'll figure it out in time."

———

EITHER CRYSTAL WAS WRONG, or Dwayne Mudd didn't have enough time. He was still stubbornly pursuing Celia when two months later, driving home from a party in what was later determined to be a condition of .12 blood-alcohol content, he turned the wrong way up a one-way street in Belgravia and collided fatally with a heavy lorry.

Celia, in the opinion of some, didn't take this news as hard as she might have—as she should have, one of them said at lunch in the canteen.

"I don't see that," protested Crystal loyally. "I know Celia was really, really shocked by what happened to Dwayne."

"Well, we all were. I'm not claiming she doesn't feel as bad as we do. But she ought to feel worse. After all, she was going out with him."

"Yes, but she's been going out with a lot of other men too, you know. Three at least."

Crystal's friends nodded. Oh, they knew that, they said crossly.

"I don't see how she can just go on as if nothing had happened," one complained. "As if she didn't really care."

Celia does too care, Crystal thought. She's still wearing Dwayne Mudd's mother's gold watch; doesn't that prove it?

IT WAS TRUE that Celia was wearing the watch. After Dwayne died she'd asked herself if perhaps she should return it—but to whom? Dwayne had no brothers or sisters; she'd have to ask someone at the embassy who his legal heirs were, which meant appearing in the embarrassing and false public role of grieving girlfriend. Possibly Dwayne had some cousin who would want the watch, but that wasn't likely. Most people—especially people in Iowa, was the thought that crossed Celia's mind, though she quickly suppressed it as snobbish—wouldn't appreciate Dwayne's mother's watch. They'd think it old-fashioned and inconvenient; they'd much prefer the latest glittery Rolex that never had to be wound and would tell them the day of the month and the time in Hong Kong. And anyhow, wouldn't Dwayne have wanted her to have it, if he'd known—?

A MONTH LATER, as if the Fates had finally harkened to Crystal's friends, Celia abruptly removed herself from competition: not by accepting another of her current beaus, but by requesting and receiving a job transfer. What amazed everyone was her destination: a small hot West African country of no political importance.

"Of course it's a fairly responsible position: Cultural Affairs Officer," a secretary in the department involved reported to her friends later in the canteen. "And the salary is good, because it's a hardship post."

"But gee, really: Goto," Crystal exclaimed.

"I know. Nobody's ever heard of it. My boss told Celia that if she'd just hang on awhile he could probably find her something much better. But Celia said she wanted to leave as soon as possible. I don't get it."

"Maybe it's because of Dwayne Mudd," suggested another young woman. "Maybe she can't forget him as long as she's here in London. She might feel guilty, even."

"I don't know," Crystal said. "Guilty doesn't exactly sound like her."

All the same, she thought later, there was definitely something on Celia's mind. She had a new distracted manner, a kind of preoccupation— Could she have realized that she'd been in love with Dwayne after all?

"I THINK I CAN GUESS why you asked for a transfer," Crystal said when Celia took her for a farewell lunch at Wheeler's. "It was because of Dwayne Mudd."

Celia started as if she'd taken hold of a defective electrical appliance. "How did you know?" she half-whispered, looking round the restaurant as if it were full of undercover agents. "I mean, what makes you say that?" she amended, recovering her cool.

"It's—well, the way you've been sort of tense ever since he died," Crystal said. "I figured you might still be thinking about Dwayne, and kind of, you know, imagining him everywhere in London."

"Yes," Celia said after a considerable pause. She lowered her fork, speared a slice of cucumber, raised it. "Not everywhere," she added, addressing the cucumber. "I only see him at certain times. . . . Whenever I'm, you know, with somebody else."

"You mean, in your mind's eye," Crystal said, stirring her salad for concealed bits of shrimp.

"What?" Celia lowered the fork again.

"I mean you don't, like, really see Dwayne? Not like a spirit apparition." Crystal leaned forward, her mouth half-open.

"Oh, no; of course not," Celia lied. She was reminded that Crystal, though reasonably discreet, was the daughter of small-town spiritualists and had a residual fascination with their beliefs.

THE TRUTH WAS, though, that Celia was seeing Dwayne Mudd, or something that looked a lot like him. Mostly he appeared as a sort of wavery grey semitransparent image printed on the scene like a weak carbon copy when the operator's forgotten to change the ribbon. He wasn't there all the time, only very occasionally—only, she realized after the first week, when she was alone with a man.

The first time Celia saw Dwayne she was in a taxi with a handsome, slightly stupid young merchant banker. As he bent and kissed her, she imagined or perceived something like Dwayne Mudd sitting on the jump seat. She sat up abruptly, and it vanished.

It was dusk, and raining, and Celia attributed the illusion to a trick of the wet half-light. But she couldn't really get into it again with the merchant banker, and when they reached her flat in Knightsbridge she checked her little gold watch, exclaimed at the lateness of the hour, and didn't ask him in.

The next time Dwayne Mudd appeared was worse, because it was daylight. Celia was on a Sunday outing with an American legal expert called Clark. They were sitting in a little wood at the top of Hampstead Heath, looking out through a stand of ancient beeches at a Constable landscape of towering cumulus clouds and descending fields of grass and flowers. Celia had just had a first-rate lunch and learnt several useful things about libel law; she felt pleased, at peace.

But when Clark put his arm round her and stroked her bare shoulder the grey shadow of the Wombat wavered into view beneath the branches of a nearby tree. This time what she saw was difficult to explain as a trick of the light: it was clearly the two-dimensional image of a man; not grey now, but weakly colored like a tinted black-and-white photograph.

"What is it?" Clark asked, following her start and fixed stare.

"I heard thunder," Celia said, improvising. "We'd better get back, we'll be drenched."

When Clark, clearly much disappointed and even cross, had returned Celia to her flat and not been invited in, she poured herself a vodka and grapefruit juice and sat down to face the situation.

She refused to consider Crystal's idea that what she had seen was a "spirit apparition," i.e. a ghost. Not only did ghosts not exist, the very idea of them was in bad taste; it went with woozy New Age music, the fingering of greasy tarot cards, and the search for people's former incarnations, who somehow always turned out to be upscale or celebrity personages.

No, there was no ghost, Celia said to herself. Rather, for some reason, she was psychologically haunted by the death of Dwayne Mudd, about which she consciously felt only a mild sadness, and also—for Dwayne had become quite a nuisance in the final month or so—a little relief.

But, Celia thought, there must be more going on subconsciously. I must believe that if I'd agreed to marry Dwayne he wouldn't be dead. Some irrational, infantile part of me must think that if I'd gone to that stuffy dinner party with him he wouldn't have drunk too much, and there wouldn't have been an accident. That's what he would probably want me to think if he were alive.

Don't be Silly, she told herself sharply, capitalizing the adjective, which had been her nickname as a small child— perhaps on the principle of opposites, for if there was anything Celia hadn't been for a long while, it was silly. That's total nonsense about Dwayne, it's just what something neurotic in you imagines. Maybe you ought to see a shrink.

But almost as rapidly as this idea came to Celia she rejected it. She couldn't afford private therapy; she'd have to go through the embassy medical plan. And when anyone did that it got into their medical records and stayed there. Of course no one was supposed to know what was in the records; but people often did know, because someone had to file them.

And when you came up for promotion, it usually came out. Then, even if there'd only been a minor problem— insomnia, for instance, or fear of flying, it could hurt your career. And hers wasn't a minor problem: she was having what a shrink would call delusions. Possibly she was actually coming down with a full-blown psychosis.

Celia, who up to now had always taken her mental stability for granted, began to feel depressed and even frightened. But she was a young woman of considerable courage and determination. The only thing to do, she finally decided, was to ignore her hallucinations and assume they would eventually go away.

An opportunity to test this theory appeared the following weekend. Celia was at home, making lunch for a former lover from America, a painter named Nat. She knew, and he knew, that this lunch would probably end in bed, for old times' sake. But as she was adding fresh cream to the vichyssoise, Nat came up close behind and embraced her; and there was the greyish shape of Dwayne Mudd again, sliding about on the sunlit wall among the shadows of the hanging Swedish ivy. As Nat caressed her right breast the shape seemed to grow darker.

"No," she said aloud.

"Sorry, love." Nat grinned. "Okay, I'll leave you alone while you cook."

The shadow wavered, faded. But it reappeared after lunch as Celia stood to clear the table.

"I've missed you," Nat said, standing also, looking directly at her.

"Yes." They moved toward each other and then, entwined, toward the bedroom. Dwayne's image followed them from room to room, sliding over the walls and furniture.

As they sank down on the bed, Celia deliberately shut her eyes. "You want to watch, Wombat, go ahead," she told him silently in her mind, where of course he was located.

As if she had spoken, a voice—Dwayne Mudd's voice, though flatter now, deadpan—in fact, dead—replied. —That's a filthy person you're with, it said. —Literally. He hasn't had a shower since Thursday.

Celia, with considerable effort, did not look round or

even open her eyes. It was clear that Nat had heard nothing, for he went on kissing her enthusiastically. She cooperated, holding him close, although now his light-brown hair had an—imagined?—odor of stale turpentine.

—You like dirt and paint, look at his hands, Dwayne Mudd's voice said. —And wait till you smell how long he's been wearing those socks.

You're lying, Celia thought, but in spite of herself she glanced at Nat's hand as it lifted her grey silk Nicole Farhi jersey. There was a sour-green smudge across the knuckles, and the square-cut nails were black. And when, in spite of her resolution, she raised her eyes, there was the shadow of Dwayne Mudd in the desk chair. Irrationally, because he was merely a figment of her imagination, she felt deeply embarrassed that he, fully clothed, should see her lying there naked.

The event that followed, though clearly great fun for Nat, was unsatisfactory to Celia. She concentrated on keeping her eyes shut, but she couldn't help hearing the voice.

—Well, look at that. He still doesn't wear underpants. Kind of disgusting, isn't it? Dwayne said, while Nat gasped and cried out, "Oh, love!"

—And get a whiff of those armpits. That was why you broke up with him, wasn't it?

"Celia, my darling," Nat murmured, subsiding, then turning to look at her. "Are you all right?" he asked. "I mean, is something the matter? You didn't— You usually—"

"I'm fine," Celia assured him. "That was lovely. But I think. . . . Well, the thing is," she continued, "I'm rather involved with someone else just now."

"Really? Oh, hell," Nat said.

THAT WAS HOW IT BEGAN; and it rapidly became worse. Soon, whenever Celia even shook hands with a man, the wavering image of Dwayne Mudd appeared and spoke. In life the Wombat's language had been decorous; now it was coarse.

—He's got zits on his ass.

—Notice how he stinks of stale smoke, from his lousy nicotine habit. Shit, you can smell it, you're close enough.

—How can you stand that mustache, so red and bristly, like a hog I knew in Iowa. Got a face like a goddamn hog, too, hasn't he?

—I suppose you know he's fucking the wife of the MP from that place in Surrey where he lives.

This last remark was directed at the merchant banker, whom Celia had been spending most of her time with lately —not because she liked him best but because he was the most imperceptive of her suitors and thus least apt to notice her distracted condition. But after she'd made discreet inquiries and discovered that Dwayne was right about the MP's wife, she crossed the banker off her list. Someone must have mentioned the affair and I must have remembered it subconsciously, she told herself. But she wasn't sure; she wasn't sure of anything anymore.

I'm falling apart, Celia thought. I've got to get out of London before I completely crack up. No, out of England.

WHEN SHE FIRST HEARD of Goto, Celia had seen in her mind a comic-book panorama of jungle and swamp, crocodiles, giant snakes, political violence, and malarial heat. But in fact it wasn't bad. Though she arrived in July the temperature was tolerable. The heavy rains had passed, and the landscape was densely green, layered like a Henri Rousseau painting with palms and banana trees and tall grasses studded with red and magenta and white flowers. The atmosphere at the embassy was agreeable and relaxed, and there was an Olympic-size outdoor pool embraced by blossoming shrubs.

Popti, the capital, turned out to be a seaside city of broad boulevards and red sandy alleys; of low blonde and ocher and terra-cotta houses and shops, with here and there a shimmering high-rise hotel or bank. For years it had been a French colony; French was still the official language, and there were visible survivals of French cuisine and French fashion.

There might be advantages in a place like this, Celia realized. She could practice her French, and develop some regional expertise. Moreover, her professional situation was greatly improved; she had an office of her own, a secretary, and the occasional use of an embassy car and driver. She also had authority; she could cause events to happen. In just a month she'd started two film series; she was reorganizing the library and negotiating with USIS in Washington for interesting speakers.

What's more, she had been assigned a four-bedroom air-conditioned villa with cook, cleaner, part-time gardener, and twenty-four-hour guard service. It was not far from the embassy, and next door to the home and shop of the city's most fashionable dressmaker, Madame Miri (to some of her European clients, Madame Marie). Celia's own house was usually quiet except for the faint, almost domestic hum of the radio that would communicate instantly with the Marine guard station at the embassy in case of emergency.

But there was always something going on in Madame's deep, leafy compound, which besides the shop contained five buildings and a large and shifting population of relatives and employees, from infants in cotton hip slings to toothless grandmothers. Celia was becoming quite friendly with Madame, who like herself was a perfectionist where dress was concerned; she had already copied a complex Issey Miyake for Celia in a remarkable black-and-indigo-grey local batik.

Most restful of all, Celia hadn't seen Dwayne Mudd

since she arrived. That proved nothing, though, for as yet she had touched no man except to shake hands. Now that she had her life organized, she knew, it was time to test her safety—her sanity, really. Because what was the alternative? The alternative was a possibly lifelong nervous celibacy.

As a sympathetic listener, Celia had not only rapidly become popular in the European community, she had acquired two admirers. She decided to go out with the one she liked least, an Oklahoma businessman—probably married, she guessed, though he claimed not—called Gary Mumpson. She therefore allowed Gary to take her to the most expensive French restaurant and, after dinner, to drive to the beach and park. It was pitch dark there, under a sky of intense tropical blackness speckled with stars. As Gary leant over to kiss her, rather sweatily, Celia held her breath. For a moment nothing happened; then, mixed with the sound of the heavy, treacherous surf, she seemed to discern an unmistakable voice.

—Yeah, give the creep a big hug, it said, so you can feel that rubber tire.

You're imagining things, Celia told herself; but her arms were already around Gary and she could not help following the Wombat's instructions.

—Anyhow, you're wasting your time, the voice seemed to say. —Not only is he married, his cock is only three inches long.

No, it was no use. "Come on, let's drive back," Celia said miserably, struggling upright.

"Nah, what for— Oh, sure. Great idea!" Gary panted, imagining (mistakenly) that this was an invitation to Celia's apartment.

THE NEXT DAY was Saturday. Celia, after a sleepless night, left her house in the hope of jogging off some of her depression. The morning was cool and fresh, the street nearly empty, but as she reached the gate of the compound next door she was greeted by Madame Miri.

In the strong sunlight her landlady was an imposing figure. Her skin shone like polished mahogany, and she wore a brilliant ballooning orange robe and turban printed with blue birds of paradise.

"What is it, *chérie?*" she inquired in her excellent French, putting a broad vermilion-nailed hand on Celia's arm.

"What?" Celia said stupidly. "What is what?"

"You are troubled this morning."

"No, not at all." Celia tried to make her voice light and unconcerned.

Madame shook her head. "I see it, in the air around you. Please, come into the shop." She lifted a hanging curtain printed with giant golden flowers.

Blurrily, Celia followed. Madame Miri indicated that she should seat herself beside the big cutting table heaped with fashion magazines and bolts of multicolored cloth, and brought her a cup of scalding French coffee.

"You don't sleep well last night," Madame Miri stated rather than inquired.

"Not very well, no," Celia admitted.

"You have the nightmare, perhaps?"

"Well, yes, sometimes," said Celia, thinking that the appearances of Dwayne Mudd were a kind of nightmare.

"I shall give you something." Madame Miri rose and swept through another curtain at the dim back of the room, where she seemed to be opening drawers and unscrewing bottles, murmuring to herself in a singsong.

I'm not going to swallow any strange medicine, Celia promised herself.

"*Voilà.*" Returning, Madame laid before Celia a small bag of reddish homespun tied with a strip of leather.

"Take this, *chérie*. You don't open it, but tonight you put it under your pillow, yes?"

"All right," Celia promised, relieved. She knew or could guess what was in the bag: a selection of the magical and medicinal herbs and bits of bone sold at stalls in the village markets and even here in the capital. It was what people called a *gris-gris*—a protective charm.

"It's good," Madame urged, smiling, holding out the little bag. "Good against fear."

Of course Madame Miri believes in spirits, she thought; almost everyone does here. The principal religion of Goto, after all, was animism: the worship of ancestors and of certain trees, rivers, and mountains. Ghosts and demons inhabited the landscape, and the fields and groves often displayed, instead of a scarecrow, a bundle of leaves and powders and bones given power by spells and hung from a branch or wedged into the fork of a tree. According to local belief, it protected the crops not only against birds and animals but against thieves and evil spirits.

"Thank you," Celia said.

When she could Celia kept her promises. She therefore put the *gris-gris* under her pillow that night, and because of it or not, slept more easily the rest of the week. Somewhat revived in spirits, she decided to risk going out with the second of her current admirers, the Marine master sergeant in charge of the guard at the embassy. Jackson was an amusing young Southerner of considerable native wit who looked well in his uniform and magnificent in swim trunks. On the down side, he was four years younger than Celia, badly educated, and had terrible political convictions.

This did not surprise Celia: in her opinion, many people had peculiar views. But however much she might disagree, she made no attempt to protest or correct them. She'd always disliked argument, which in her experience never convinced anyone—only facts did that, and even then not very often. Whenever she seriously disagreed with someone she repeated a phrase her father had taught her when she was fourteen: "You may be right." ("It took me fifty-five years to learn to say that," he had told her. "Maybe it'll save you a little trouble.")

At the last moment before Jackson arrived in his red Corvette, Celia, with a superstitious impulse of which she was rather ashamed, placed Madame Miri's *gris-gris* in the bottom of her handbag. But when her date handed—or, more accurately, handled—her into the car, she thought for a moment that she saw Dwayne's image, wavering but distinct, on the whitewashed wall of the compound. It was transformed almost at once into the blowing shadows of a banyan tree, and Celia scolded herself for succumbing to nerves.

Unlike Gary, Jackson did not wait to make his move till after supper. As soon as they pulled up in front of the open-air restaurant, from which noisy, thumping local music was soaking, he turned toward Celia. "Hey, you really look super tonight," he said, grabbing her expertly.

Dwayne Mudd reappeared at once, sitting on the hood of the Corvette: strangely grey and semitransparent against the sun-flooded tropical shrubbery, as if the light that shone on him was still the humid grey light of London—but unmistakable. —You better watch your step with this one, he announced.

"Oh, shut up," Celia said silently. "I've come all this way; I'm going to enjoy myself if I feel like it."

—He goes with whores, Dwayne continued relentlessly, pressing his grey face up against the windshield. —You should find out when he was last tested for AIDS. And check if he has a cut on his lip.

Involuntarily, Celia ran the tip of her tongue over Jackson's wide mouth. Mistaking her intention, he gasped and pulled her closer, murmuring, "Oh, baby."

THAT NIGHT, oppressed by both anxiety and frustrated desire, Celia slept worse than ever—as was immediately apparent to Madame Miri when she appeared next morning.

"But it is not yet well, *ma petite,*" she announced, after lowering herself into a chair and accepting coffee.

"No," Celia admitted. "I guess your charm doesn't work on Europeans." She laughed nervously.

Madame ignored this. "There is something heavy on your mind, is it not so?" she asked.

"No— Well, yes." Giving in, Celia told Madame Miri, gradually, everything. She'll know I'm insane now, she thought as the grotesque words fell from her mouth like the toads and snakes of the old fairy tale. She'll tell me to see a doctor.

"My poor child," Madame said instead, when Celia fell nervously silent. "I see how it is. This individual, he is jealous. Since he cannot have you, he wants to keep all other men away. That I have seen before, *eh oui.*" She sighed. "And so for nothing you made this long journey." For the first time, she used the intimate second person singular. "Though perhaps not for nothing," she added almost to herself.

"I thought, if I was so far from London—"

"*Chérie,* two, three thousand miles, they are like this" (she snapped her fingers) "to a spirit. They don't figure space like we do."

"A spirit?" Celia echoed.

"*Exactement.*" Madame Miri smiled, and Celia remembered a verse from a tribal chant that had been recited to her by the Deputy Chief of Mission, a former anthropologist:

Those who are dead have not gone.
They are in the shadow that brightens,

They are in the shadow that fades,
They are in the shadow that trembles.

"And how was he called in life, this *personnage?*" Madame asked.

"Dwayne Mudd," Celia said.

Madame frowned. "Mudd. *C'est la boue, n'est-ce pas?*"

"Yes, I suppose so," Celia admitted.

"A bad name. Ill-omened."

"Evidently," Celia said. She tried an uneasy laugh, but Madame ignored the pathetic result.

"It takes a spirit to catch a spirit," she said in a low voice, leaning across the table toward Celia as if Dwayne Mudd might be listening. "You know perhaps some very powerful woman gone over to the other side, your mother, your grandmother *peut-être?*"

Celia shook her head. "No, I'm sorry. They're both still alive. And my other grandmother, my father's mother—I don't know. I never liked her much, and I don't think she liked me either." She looked up at Madame Miri, who was still waiting patiently, and then down into the dark reflections of her coffee cup.

"There is someone," she said after a pause. "I never knew her, but I'm named after her. She was my father's stepmother."

"Une belle-mère, mais sympathique."

"Oh yes, so my father claims. He never uses the word 'wonderful' about anyone or anything, but he said once that she was a wonderful woman— I'm supposed to be like her, even though we weren't related."

"That's well. Perhaps you have her soul."

"Maybe," Celia said, recalling that according to local belief ancestral spirits returned after death to inhabit their newborn descendants.

"En tout cas, she's without doubt watching over you, or

you would not have thought of her now." Madame Miri smiled.

"I'm not so sure about that," Celia said. "I mean, if she is, I guess she hasn't been watching very often, or I wouldn't be in this fix now."

"Pas certain, chérie. This *belle-mère,* she was perhaps a very polite lady?"

"What?" Celia asked, feeling disoriented. Lack of sleep, she thought. "Oh, yes. My father said she had perfect manners."

"That explains it. She's watching over you, *oui,* but when you and some type are becoming close" (Madame made a somewhat obscene gesture) *"elle est bien élevée,* she averts her eyes. And, *tu me l'as raconté,* that's the only time this evil spirit appears."

"Yes," Celia agreed. Am I really having this conversation? she thought.

"Very well. I tell you, this is what you do. Next time you see him, you call for *la belle-mère.* Not necessary to shout her name out loud, just whisper in your mind, '*Venez, venez à moi, aidez-moi.'* "

"All right," Celia promised.

FOR A FEW MINUTES after Madame Miri had left, she felt better. Perhaps she wasn't mad after all, only haunted. In Goto the existence of supernatural beings did not seem so impossible. Out in the country, almost every village was guarded by one or more fetish figures, which resembled large grey stone fire hydrants hung with colored rags and garlands of flowers. They had broad faces, staring eyes, and huge sexual organs, and gave off, even to a skeptic like Celia, an ominous and powerful aura.

Even here in the capital, the totemic animal of the dominant local tribe, the pigeon, was honored by a monumental sculpture of a huge white bird, described in tourist brochures as the "Pigeon of Peace." Closer at hand, in a shadowy corner of Madame Miri's courtyard, squatted two household gods, smaller versions of the village fetish figures. They wore bright, constantly renewed garlands of red and orange flowers, and each day Madame's cook fed them: their open stone mouths were always smeared with dried blood and rice and fruit pulp.

But Celia's euphoria lasted only briefly. She realized that if she began to take all this seriously she would be mentally worse off than before: not only having delusions, but starting to believe in ghosts, and thinking that she could exorcise them by invoking the name of an ancestor whom she had never met and who wasn't even an ancestor. Going native, in fact, she thought. She had already heard stories about people, anthropologists mostly, who began by taking the local belief system too seriously and ended up partly or wholly off their rockers.

Some of these tales, and most of the information about Gotolese superstition, had come from a man in whom Celia was becoming seriously interested: the Deputy Chief of Mission himself, a young career diplomat and former anthropologist named Charles Fenn. He was a tall, thin, very intelligent, slightly odd-looking man about forty, with a long face, skewed eyebrows, a beaky nose, and a satirical, melancholy manner. She had liked him from the start, without ever thinking of him as a possible beau. But then, everyone at the embassy liked Charles, from the ambassador (a fat, elderly Texan magnate whose contributions to the Republican party had earned him this honorary post) down to the twelve-year-old Gotolese undergardener.

According to embassy gossip, melancholy was not Charles's normal mood, but the result of events beyond his control. He was recently separated and in the process of being divorced: his ex-wife, everyone said, had been a cute and even lovable airhead, but terminally indiscreet and totally unable to adjust to West Africa. Since she left, Charles had been under the weather emotionally, while remaining unvaryingly hardworking and sympathetic to his staff. "He really listens to you," people often said.

"Yes, I know," Celia always replied, feeling mildly uneasy, because this was what people often said about her.

Her unease escalated to panic at her next one-to-one meeting with Charles, after her skilled attentiveness had drawn him into describing his years as an anthropologist.

"It's a very cluttered field," he was telling her. "In more ways than one. You know what they say about the Navaho, that the typical family consists of a grandparent, the parents, 3.2 children, and an anthropologist. It was almost like that where I was. I realized I wasn't only going to be unnecessary and ineffectual, I was going to be superfluous."

"Tell me more," Celia murmured encouragingly as he paused and gazed out the window into the glossy green crown of an embassy avocado tree.

Charles turned and looked at her. "You always say that, don't you?" he remarked with what struck Celia as a dangerous casualness. " 'Tell me more.' "

"No—well, not always," she stammered.

Charles smiled. "Or else you say, 'That's really interesting.' Persuading the other person to go on talking, so you'll get to know them, and they won't know you. I recognize the technique, you see, because I do it too."

"I don't . . ." Celia began, and swallowed the rest of the fib.

"But now I think it's your turn. *You* tell *me* more." He did not take his eyes off her. They were a strange color, she saw, between dark gold and green.

"More about what?"

"I don't care. Your childhood, your opinions, your ambitions, your dreams, whatever you like. As long as it's the truth, of course." Charles smiled.

"I—uh." Celia hesitated; her heart seemed to flop in her chest like a fish.

"I know. Tell me about your time in the Peace Corps, what you liked most about that." He glanced at the wall clock. "You have ten minutes, all right?"

"All right," Celia said. She swallowed. "I think it was the way the villages looked at night," she was surprised to hear herself say. "Especially when there was a moon . . ." Why did I agree? she asked herself. Why didn't I just laugh it off and say Not today or I don't feel like it? I could still say that. But instead she heard her voice going on, beginning to speak of things she'd not told anyone, not because they were private or shocking, but because nobody had ever really listened, they were all just waiting their turn to talk—

It's the way he looks at me, she thought, glancing at Charles. He knows I'm here. Is that how I make people feel?

"That's very interesting," Charles said as she paused, glancing at the clock and then back at Celia. "Go on."

"Well. It's because, you see, the desert isn't quiet at night. There are all the sounds in the trees and scrub outside the village, rustlings and squeaks and sighs, and you're there, you're part of it . . . you feel . . ." She looked at Charles Fenn. He was still listening; he heard her, every word. This could be important, she thought. It is important.

She thought it again after she left Charles's office, and that evening back home. She told herself that Charles was a most unusual man. That without his flighty wife he would probably go far; with Celia, even farther—if she were ever her normal self again. Otherwise she would simply screw up his career, not to mention her own, she thought wretchedly. Then she reminded herself that there was no reason to worry about this, because nothing Charles had yet done or said suggested he wanted to go anywhere with her. But for some reason that made Celia feel even more miserable.

Things were still in this condition when Charles asked Celia to accompany him and another staff member to a reception at the French Embassy. The commercial attaché was in the front seat with the driver; Charles and Celia in the back, and as they drove through streets illuminated by the mauve and vermilion afterglow of a tropical sunset Charles described the rank, history, and personal peculiarities of the people she was about to meet.

"There's a lot of rather odd characters in the local diplomatic corps, I'm afraid," he concluded. "But I hope you're going to like it here all the same." The car lurched suddenly round a corner, flinging Celia, in her gossamer-light pale-mauve muslin dress, abruptly against him.

"Thanks, I think I will," she replied distractedly, trying to catch her breath, not moving away.

"I'm very glad to hear that." Charles also did not move; under the cover of the attaché case on his lap, he put his hand on hers.

—You're making another mistake, said the flat dead voice of Dwayne Mudd. At first Celia could not see him; then she realized he was sitting, grey and squeezed up, between Charles and the door.

—You think he's so fucking great. He's got—

I don't want to hear it, Celia thought desperately, feeling the steady, disturbing, desirable pressure of Charles's shoulder, arm, and hand against hers.

—athlete's foot, and—

Remembering Madame Miri, she cried out silently in her mind to the other Celia Zimmern. *Venez à moi, aidez-moi!* How stupid it sounded: like calling on herself.

Miraculously, the horrible flat voice ceased. My God, it worked, Celia thought. But the shadow of Dwayne Mudd did not vanish: it remained in the car, silently moving its greyish lips, until they reached the French Embassy.

"SO, HOW DOES IT GO?" Madame Miri asked next morning, waylaying Celia as she went out for an early run. Narrowing her eyes in the brilliant sun, she added, "Perhaps not completely well, yes?"

"He's still there," Celia admitted. "I can't hear him anymore, but he's there, trying to speak, opening and shutting his mouth. Half the way to the French Embassy yesterday evening in the car, and all the way back— Well, whenever I— You know. I can't bear it anymore!" she cried suddenly. "I think I'm going mad."

"Ah, no, *chérie*. Come, come *chez moi*. We must consider further about this."

In a dazed condition, weakened by another night without sleep, Celia followed Madame to her shop and then, for the first time, through the curtain into the back room. It was low, dimly lit, hung with thick woven and embroidered fabrics and dominated by a kind of altar covered with an embroidered red cloth and crowded with flowers and images, including what looked like a lion with wings.

"Sit down, please." Madame Miri indicated a low multicolored leather pouf.

"There is something," she said, opening her eyes after some moments of silent concentration. "I think this spirit of mud has got some hold on you."

"I don't know—" Celia said. "Maybe I feel guilty—"

"Guilty, that is nothing. This is not your husband, only a stupid, jealous spirit. But I think perhaps there is some object that he has given to you, and through this he has power to come to you when he desires."

Involuntarily, Celia glanced at her left wrist; at Dwayne's mother's gold watch. Madame Miri followed her gaze. "So that is his?" she asked.

"Yes. Well, it was his mother's."

"So, even worse. In it, her power is joined to his. I understand well now." She nodded several times.

"You think I shouldn't wear this watch when I go out with someone?"

"Never you should wear it," Madame said solemnly. "It is dangerous to you always. Give it to me; I will take care of it."

Somewhat stunned by this development, Celia did not move.

"You must hold to persons, not to things," said Madame Miri, putting out her hand.

Slowly, Celia unfastened the gold mesh band and placed her Cartier watch in Madame's broad black-rimmed apricot-tinted palm, where it looked strangely small.

"But if it's so dangerous—" she said, watching what she had come to think of as her property disappear into Madame's fist. "I mean, if you have the watch, won't he come to you?"

Madame Miri laughed. "If he comes, let him come. He will have a large surprise, will he not?" She laughed again, more fully. "Don't derange yourself, *ma petite,*" she said gently. "I know how to deal with such as him, *je te le jure.*"

FIVE MONTHS LATER, Celia Zimmern and Charles Fenn were married in the garden of the American Embassy in Goto. There were well over a hundred guests; strings of colored lanterns—ruby, sapphire, topaz, and jade-green— laced the tropical evening; fireworks were set off beside the pool. Madame Miri, who had created Celia's spectacular white tulle and lace wedding dress from a Givenchy pattern, sat at one end of the long head table, resplendent in vermilion silk brocaded in gold, with a matching fantastically folded headdress.

"A day of joy," she said when Celia, circulating among the company, stopped beside her. "I see that all is well with you."

"Oh, yes." Celia looked at Madame again. On both

broad, glowing mahogany arms she wore a mass of gold bangles; among them was the gold Cartier watch. But that's mine, Celia wanted to say; then she faltered, realizing that the statement was false, and that anyhow this was the wrong time and place for it; that perhaps there would never be a right time or place.

Madame Miri, unembarrassed, followed the direction of her gaze. "That one has not appeared again to you, *n'est-ce pas?*"

"No, not since—" Celia glanced at her own slim wrist, on which there was now only a faint band of untanned skin. Out of practical necessity she had purchased a Timex from the embassy commissary, but usually kept it in her handbag. "Has he appeared to you?" she added, registering the emphasis in Madame's phrasing.

"*Ah oui;* I have seen him, with his little mustache," replied Madame Miri. "A good appearance, that fellow. But not interesting, no. *Jamais.* Not like that man of yours there, eh?" She gave an intimate laugh, bubbly with champagne, and gestured toward Charles, who was also moving among the guests.

"No," Celia said, trying to remember if she had ever told Madame Miri that the Wombat had a small mustache. She knew she had told Charles; indeed, a month ago, without really intending to do so, she had found herself telling Charles everything about Dwayne Mudd.

His reaction, as always, was interested and sympathetic. "I think most people see their former lovers sometimes, though not as clearly as you did. I used to see my wife; almost see her anyhow. And if you live in a place like this for a while you're not surprised by anything."

Somehow after that Celia had at last succeeded in forgetting Dwayne Mudd. But now, dizzied by happiness and champagne, she imagined him as a fretful ghost eternally bound to Goto, a country he would probably have deplored and detested—he hated what he called "the sticks." She even wondered if he were present this evening, invisible and inaudible except to Madame Miri.

"Do you think Dwayne's at the party, then?" she asked, glancing round uneasily, and then back at Madame Miri. In the jeweled light of the paper lanterns Madame looked larger and more formidable than ever. What she really resembled, Celia thought, was the female of the pair of larger-than-life mahogany figures in the local museum. Heavy-limbed, heavy-lidded, they had been roughly carved a century or more ago; they were identified on their label as *Gardes des portes de l'enfer*—guardians of the gates of Hell.

"No." Madame Miri shook her turbaned head slowly, so that her heavy earrings swayed. "He is not here." She was no longer laughing. "He has gone where he should go." She pointed down, toward the earth. But then she smiled and raised her glass. "Do not think more of him, *chérie*," she told Celia. "He will not trouble you again."

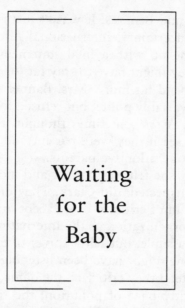

Waiting
for the
Baby

HERE IN NEW DELHI at the end of their long quest,
waiting day after day for International Adoption Services to find them a baby, Aster was finally losing heart. At
home in America she and her husband Clark had spoken of
the coming journey as not only a necessary mission, but a
chance to tour the country and learn more about their future child's culture.

But none of the books and articles she had read had pre-
pared Aster for India: its crazy contrasts of beauty and hid-
eousness, luxury and poverty, friendly simplicity and im-
penetrable evasiveness. Also, nobody had told them that
May was intolerably hot, the worst season for travel. Shopping and sightseeing were possible only in the mornings;
after lunch, if they didn't have to go to the agency, Aster
and Clark stayed in the air-conditioned hotel or, as now, in
its big outdoor pool.

One after another, they had canceled their trips to Jaipur,

Jodhpur, Agra, and Benares. It wasn't just the heat, it was the economic uncertainty. International Adoption Services still hadn't come up with a final statement of costs or a definite date; they might have to stay far longer than they'd planned, and spend far more. Mrs. Bannerjee and her colleagues were invariably polite, but refused to commit themselves. Perhaps, Aster sometimes thought, the agency was testing them to see if they were patient and even-tempered enough to be good adoptive parents.

But every day she felt less patient and more stressed out —and so, she suspected, did Clark. They didn't admit this to each other, didn't criticize IAS, except once when Clark referred to the organization as the International Asses. (Aster had flicked a smile, but felt a shiver of fear, as if something or someone might have been listening and would report them.) Instead they criticized the damp, leaden heat of the city, the gritty haze of pollution; the riotous, reckless traffic; the overspiced, possibly spoilt food—for days now Aster had felt a little nauseous—and the terrifying poverty. Along Janpath tall banks and office buildings shimmered in the sun, and satiny tropical flowers poured over their walls; but below, bundles of rags that on second glance were people lay in dust and vomit, coughing and dying.

At first she had found the Red Fort and the other ancient monuments and temples fascinating; but gradually they began to seem dusty and worn, as if their surfaces had been pitted by too many staring tourist eyes. In the narrow soiled alleys of Old Delhi a dog pissed on her skirt; and when she rinsed out the new silk scarf she had spilt coffee on, its exotic colors ran into a muddy brown.

It was probably because she was in such an exhausted, keyed-up state that a few days ago Aster had made a fool of herself at one of the local sights. She had gone there on impulse late one afternoon, because it was near the public library where Clark was absorbed in back issues of American newspapers.

The Birla Mandir temple hadn't ever been on their must-see list. It dated only from 1938, and Aster knew already from her guidebook that it would be banal rather than beautiful: an oriental film-fantasy edifice, all balconies and galleries and stairs in marble the color and texture of banana ice cream.

As usual, she had to leave her shoes at a stall by the entrance. But this time she hadn't worn socks, and the yellow marble steps were scorching under her bare feet and also filthy: littered with the fading, slimy remnants of orange and yellow garlands of marigolds and sticky pink sweets.

With the help of the guidebook she had now identified the most popular Hindu deities: the trinity of Brahma, Vishnu, and Shiva; elephant-headed Ganesh, who favored all new enterprises; graceful Saraswati, patroness of the arts; and the frolicsome blue youth Krishna. It had seemed a benevolent ancient pantheon, and one that acknowledged the power of the female.

But in this bright, modern edifice, which reminded Aster of brochures for the Indian palace hotels they couldn't afford, the gods were not museum-quality statues softened by time, but glaringly new, like Disney figures. They were overdressed, and decorated in the worst of taste with gold leaf and costume jewelry. Some were pretty in the artificial manner of Indian advertisements; others had the heads of animals, necklaces of flowers and skulls, or faces black with rage; they showed pointed teeth and waved extra arms holding the weapons of war. Like the life-size Mickey and Minnie Mice at Disneyland, they suggested vulgar commercial power.

Early evening is the traditional time of worship in India, and these half-comic, half-sinister deities basked in the light of many candles; thick, odorous, dizzying smoke shrouded them, and an increasing crowd of devotees stood or knelt before the shrines. Several of these worshippers gave Aster hard looks as she tried to maneuver between them for a better view of Lakshmi, to whom (according to her guidebook) the temple was dedicated, and one woman even muttered what sounded like a curse.

"Goddess of fortune and abundance," Aster read in her guidebook. "Lakshmi gives wealth, fertility, and many children." I'll settle for the one we've been promised, she thought. Lakshmi, who had four arms and sat between two elephants, was heavily jeweled and voluptuous of figure, with the swelling breasts and stomach of a woman in the early stages of pregnancy. She had dark-rimmed almond eyes, an ivory complexion, and a little sly smile. "Nyah, nyah," she seemed to be saying to Aster. "I know something you don't know."

The Indian woman next to Aster now knelt facing the shrine, then lowered herself, breathing heavily, until she was prostrate in a puddle of red silk sari, with her heavily ringed and braceleted hands clasped above her head.

How can she do that, how can she lie there in the filth? Aster wondered. The answer sounded inside her head in a thin mosquito tone: "Because she wants a baby more than you do."

Nobody wants a baby more than I do, Aster thought angrily, nobody. And suddenly, without willing it, she found herself dropping to the smeared, dirty floor; kneeling, then actually lying prone, with her legs sticking out awkwardly behind her. Noise and incense streamed round her; time seemed to whirl.

"Please, give us our baby now," she heard herself whisper. Then, dizzy and embarrassed, she rose to her feet, glancing round, seeing or imagining the pink shocked and disapproving faces of other Westerners in the crowd of darker and more golden faces.

What a stupid, unsanitary thing to do, she thought as she hastened away from the shrine into the open air, brushing bits of debris from her stained slacks, checking her watch. It was much later than she'd thought, and behind the temple the sun was setting: rose and purple clouds, edged with gold in the worst possible taste, streaked the smoky sky.

ASTER DIDN'T TELL CLARK about what had happened at the Lakshmi temple; instead the incident added itself to the growing list of things they didn't talk about. It had begun two years ago, she thought, after they went to their first adoption agency. When they realized that they not only had to be but to act the part of perfect prospective parents. Which was the truth: they were educated, successful, healthy, attractive, decent people.

But by being consciously put forward and waved about for so long, this truth had slowly turned into a lie, at least for Aster. She knew from the start that if one of them was found wanting, it would be her. She began to have anxious, uncertain moods; she kept remembering how her mother had remarked with a gentle, dotty smile that "perhaps it wasn't meant to be." But when she told Clark this he only laughed and said, "New Age thinking."

So Aster set her doubts and questions aside, concealing them first from the social workers, then from her friends and family, finally from Clark himself. And after a while it seemed that if she admitted doubts or questions she hadn't already mentioned, it would be like admitting that she'd been deliberately deceiving everyone.

That's how it was with her insomnia, Aster thought. And her fear of Clark's parents, who once—before they knew she and Clark would have to adopt—said they didn't see how anyone could feel the same about a grandchild that didn't have their genes. Aster never said that she was worried about their attitude; more and more she didn't even tell Clark when she was ill or upset.

We're together all day here, more than we've ever been for years, she thought. But we don't really talk anymore; we haven't for a long time.

Lately, for instance, she had stopped speaking about the noises that kept her awake every night. The sullen intermittent rasp and chug of the air conditioner, the monotonous plinking and sawing of Asian music, the creak and clang of the hotel elevator. And sometimes another fainter sound: a sort of gasping whine and wail. The first time she woke Clark. "Did you hear that?" she cried.

"Wha?" In the half-light her husband, who slept easily and heavily, half-raised his head.

"There's a child crying."

"That's just air in the plumbing." He fell back into unconsciousness.

But the wailing of the ghostly child, or plumbing, continued. Aster heard it almost every night. She did not wake Clark again, because she feared he would say, as he sometimes did, smiling, "Aster's always hearing things other people can't hear." Which was not only a compliment to her aural acuity, but an oblique reference to her Southern Californian counterculture background. It was unfair, because she had long ago put all that behind her, along with her embarrassing given name, Astarte.

Indeed, it was from all that the name Astarte stood for that Aster was determined to rescue their baby. Their child, Indian though it might be genetically, would not grow up as she had, in a confused, impoverished, unhygienic world of vague spirituality and too many siblings; a world of mantras, meditation, and meaningless hugs; of faded hand-me-down skirts made of old bedspreads and spiced vegetable stew left out on the stove till it turned dry and sour; of the good-natured selfishness called "doing one's own thing."

When Aster first complained of the noises at night, she and Clark had discussed moving to a better hotel. Now, as their stack of traveler's checks flattened, she suggested a cheaper one.

"YOU KNOW that couple from Sweden we met last week at the agency," she began as they lay beside the lukewarm hotel pool, in which exotic dead insects floated.

"You mean the ones with the very dark baby." Clark's voice had the same mix of amusement and dismay as when he had first pointed out the two very tall and fair young people and their tiny, almost black infant. ("You'd think IAS would make more effort to match the child to the parents," he had commented.)

"Yes, well, they're in a three-star hotel, and she told me it's really quite all right. I thought we might call and see if they've got a room."

"I—don't know." Clark spoke in the manner he'd developed recently: short bursts of words interrupted by long pauses. Somehow it was associated in Aster's mind with the explosive sounds of the twenty-four-hour green death he'd had after eating in an outdoor restaurant, as if speech too were a painful kind of evacuation. "We'd have to tell IAS we were moving."

"Well, yes, of course."

"They might think we were—running out of money."

"Well, we are," Aster said. "At least we may if we have to stay in Delhi much longer."

"The thing is—if they thought—that we'd misrepresented—"

"But we didn't." Aster's answer was almost a question. Clark's income as a planning consultant was more mysteri-

ous and variable than hers as an arts administrator. "Did
we?"

"No—but I'd rather not take the chance." Clark did not
look at his wife as he spoke, but up into the ragged, sun-
faded palms.

But I have to move, I have to leave this expensive
haunted hotel, Aster thought. She opened her mouth to say
so, then shut it. We mustn't quarrel, she told herself, that
could ruin everything. No agency will give a baby to mutu-
ally hostile, squabbling parents. And if they did have a fight
now it could be serious, and the scars might show at their
interview later this afternoon.

"All right," she agreed, not agreeing.

Hang in there, she told herself, turning over onto her
back under the smoggy sun. It's going to work out; hadn't
Mrs. Fogel back home practically assured them of that?
"You shouldn't have any problem with IAS," she had said,
emphasizing the pronoun as if she saw a banner over Clark
and Aster's heads reading IDEAL ADOPTIVE COUPLE.

Their baby would be a girl, Aster was almost certain of
that; it was girl babies who were given away in India, or
neglected and allowed to die of fever or malnutrition. Or
deliberately destroyed before birth once their sex was
known. Aster was in favor of a woman's right to choose,
but she couldn't help thinking sometimes of the daily
waste, the loss, the murder of healthy, lovable Indian infants.

And, since Roe versus Wade, American ones. She and
Clark had been caught in a pocket of history: thirty years
ago people like them would have had their choice of babies.
One day, perhaps, the Supreme Court might overturn that
decision. But they couldn't wait that long; already she was
forty and Clark forty-one, too old for any American
agency. Because that was how those places worked; they

made you wait four years, five, six, and then said you were too old. This was their last chance.

Aster was glad it would be a girl. She didn't say so though, just as Clark didn't say any longer that he wanted a boy, as he had when they assumed it would be with them as with other couples. "Clark Stockwell IV first, and then whatever you like," he'd joked, when they still joked about such things. Perhaps even now he hoped for a boy.

How awful it was, how unfair, that they should have to sit in offices and beg favors from strangers, submit financial statements, and be inspected and judged. Meanwhile people who were unstable and irresponsible, or even cruel and crazy, had one baby after another. At home she couldn't go to the mall without seeing some angry unfit mother with several miserable unkempt children she didn't appear to want. Didn't deserve.

It was the same here: Delhi was full of ragged exhausted-looking women carrying one half-naked baby and dragging another. And then, almost worse, the child beggars: thin, dirty, barefoot, some seeming as young as four or five. Everywhere you went they crowded round you, patted your arm, fumbled at your clothes, crying "Baksheesh, baksheesh!" You couldn't know which, if any, weren't faking; the only solution was to give nothing at all.

"Remember what the guidebook said, we mustn't give them anything," she had warned Clark on their first day in Delhi, when skinny clamoring urchins surrounded them as they emerged from the airport into the choking heat.

"Sorry," he had said, following her into the taxi and slamming the door. "It was just some of those little tin coins—No, damn it, that's all."

But more and more ragged children appeared as if from nowhere, crying in their shrill voices, reaching out their thin dark hands. Even when Aster rolled up the window the children pressed their dirty faces and hands against the glass and stared at her with their liquid inky eyes until the taxi, accelerating, shook them off.

"What I don't understand is, why doesn't some agency find decent homes for some of those kids?" she had asked Clark that first evening, when they had gone for a walk along Janpath and had to turn into a souvenir shop to escape the beggars—not just children but wizened grandmothers in threadbare saris; androgynous toothless gnomes with leprosy-melted noses or hands; threatening adolescents with knife-scarred faces.

"It wouldn't be possible," Clark had said. In the harsh light of the shop, surrounded by the glitter of brass trays and bowls and candlesticks, he looked exhausted. "Children like that, nobody would want them. They have chronic diseases, bad heredity, could be retarded. Besides, most of them probably have parents already, or at least someone they belong to. Someone who teaches them to beg, lives off them."

His face took on an expression it assumed back home when a job went seriously wrong: the compressed mouth, the narrowed eyes. More and more often he wore that mask, Aster thought; he had it on now as he lay in the deck chair by the pool, his canvas cricket hat tilted to shade his eyes and his long pale legs shielded from the sun by a blue-striped hotel towel.

But it doesn't matter, she told herself. Soon, surely, they will have their baby. They will take her home to the room that is ready for her, with the big white teddy bear, the bird mobile floating over the crib. They will talk to each other again.

"IT'S GOING TO HAPPEN," Aster declared three hours later as they reentered their hotel room. "I'm sure of it."

"I hope you're right." Clark sighed. "God, I need a shower."

"Me too," she said, following him into the bathroom. "Mrs. Bannerjee smiled much more today, didn't you think?"

"She always smiles," Clark said.

"And she promised to call later with definite news." Aster peeled off her damp cotton dress and tight damp bra.

"Mm. You go first."

Clark's so cautious, she thought as she stood naked in the lukewarm spray. But I know we're going to get our baby. One child at least will be rescued from the confusion, squalor, and violence of India: her life changed forever, her future assured.

"Your turn," she said, reaching for a towel.

Though cooler than outside, the room was warm. Not bothering to put on a robe, Aster stretched out on the flower-patterned bedspread.

"That's better." Naked too, Clark sat beside her, then leaned closer. "Aster? How about it?"

"Why not?" She smiled. The one good thing about New Delhi was what it had done for their physical relationship. Six years ago, when they realized that she wasn't going to get pregnant at once, sex had gradually become a matter first of weighted meaning, later of mechanical calculation, of charts and thermometers. By the time it had been proved and proved again that all efforts were ineffectual, they were worn out, reduced to routine gestures of affection modulating occasionally into the release of tension.

But in New Delhi they had had time to rest and recover; time to experiment.

"Oh, darling," Aster whispered twenty minutes later. In spite of the air-conditioning, she was warmly damp again everywhere. "I feel so good."

"Really." Clark smiled.

"It's as if I were, I don't know, tingling all over, especially my breasts."

"Umhm. . . . Oh, hell." The phone had begun to ring beside the other twin bed; he floundered toward it.

"Clark Stockwell here. . . . Yes?" A long pause, during which he dragged the spread across his legs as if to conceal himself from the telephone's gaze. Aster raised herself on one elbow; there was a sick pain in her stomach, as of nausea.

"Yes, but I understood—" Another pause, so long this time that she sat up, then went to kneel beside him.

"No. I thought you had already approved—" Clark's voice was the formal, neutral one he used when a client ignorant of good business manners called him at home. "No, we didn't."

"What is it?" Aster cried as he replaced the receiver.

"I'm so sorry, darling." Clark cleared his throat with a raw, grating sound. "IAS has turned us down."

"No! Why?"

"They won't give any reason. Said it's against their policy." Clark cleared his throat again. "I don't know—it could be what we were worried about before, that they think we're too old."

"But that's so stupid! Mrs. Fogel said it wouldn't matter— Anyhow, America isn't India, our average life expectancy is, I don't know, seventy-five? A child born now would be over thirty by then. We have to explain, we have to tell them—"

"I don't think it'll do any good. Mrs. Bannerjee sounded very definite."

"I don't care. I'm going to call back."

Clark said neither yes nor no; he continued to sit there while Aster fought her way through the hotel switchboard and the New Delhi phone system. Unconcerned now that she might seem a hysterical, pushy, imperfect parent, she demanded to speak to everyone they'd met at IAS—protesting, arguing, begging, trying unsuccessfully to get through the screen of polite regret.

"They're all so impossible, so ignorant," she cried after she had hung up. "I hate that fat Mrs. Bannerjee, I hate every one of them." She swallowed a sob. "Listen, Clark. Why don't you call the director. Men count for more than women in this country; maybe he'll listen to you."

Her husband shook his head. "It won't do any good," he repeated.

Clark doesn't understand, she thought. And when we made love just now he didn't say he loved me. And if we don't love each other, we can't stay together after this; nobody could.

ALL THE REST of that evening, while Aster raged and wept, Clark remained frozen. He had two drinks before dinner and most of a bottle of wine, but to no discernible effect. Aster, though she drank less, soon grew unsteady. At ten she stood weeping with dizzy fury in the shower, which trickled over her as if weeping too.

"I still can't believe it, I still can't bear it," she wailed, collapsing onto her bed.

"I know, darling. I'm so sorry," Clark muttered from the other bed, his voice thick with alcohol and exhaustion. In a few minutes he was breathing heavily, regularly—almost snoring. Aster lay awake, watching the wavering light through the blinds, hearing the ugly mélange of hotel noises: the meaningless tuneless tinkling and sawing music, the groan and clank of the elevator, the faint, mocking sound like a child crying.

She slept, finally, and woke exhausted and ill. The wobbly look of the fried eggs on her plate at breakfast sickened her. When Clark volunteered to go to the travel desk and ask for plane reservations to America, she staggered back to their room and fell into a defeated daze.

Half an hour later he returned. They were lucky, they could fly home tonight, he reported; but why shouldn't they, instead, delay their departure and see more of India while they were here? Why not travel to some cool, picturesque hill station?

"Look, here's some possibilities." Clark held out a shiny colored fan of brochures. "I think we should go somewhere, so this trip won't be totally wasted."

Aster struck the brochures with the side of her hand so that they fell in disarray on the carpet. "But it is wasted," she cried. "Everything's wasted, everything we've done for years is wasted. I hate India."

"We could try Nepal, then. There's supposed to be a very good hotel in Katmandu, and at this time of year—"

"I don't want to try anywhere." Aster began to cry again, the dry, empty sobs of exhaustion. "I just want to go home."

"Oh, darling. I'm so sorry," Clark said for perhaps the third time in twenty-four hours. "Whatever you like."

Why does he keep apologizing to me? she thought after her husband had returned to the travel desk.

It's because it's worse for you, said the thin voice in her head. Because the truth is that Clark doesn't want a darkskinned Indian baby girl; he never wanted one. He's like his parents: what he wanted was a child who would look like him.

But Clark could still have what he wants, Aster thought as she began to fold clothes into her suitcase. Forty-one isn't old for a man: he could marry again and have children. She could even see the bride he would choose: one of those bright young legal aides in his office. He was a goodlooking man, well mannered, successful, intelligent. Lots of young women would be glad to marry him and produce Clark Stockwell IV.

He could have chosen one of them already, Aster

thought, opening another drawer and taking out a stack of T-shirts. But instead he stayed with me, even after he knew there would never be a real Clark Stockwell IV. He went to all those agencies and interviews with me, and came to India with me, because I wanted an Indian baby. He came for me, because he loved me.

Yes, and I love him, she thought. But what good is that? She had reached the bottom drawer now, full of the cool-weather clothes she'd never worn since they left home, and odds and ends of toiletries. A first-aid kit, a box of diapers they would never use, an unopened box of pads named Always— Why had she chosen a brand with that mocking name, a name that promised she would never get pregnant, that she would bleed every month, always, until she was too old to bleed?

Unopened? But they must have been in India nearly a month, Aster thought. She should have been off long before now. It must be the heat, the jet shock, the anxiety and misery that had delayed her period—Aster dropped an armful of clothes on the bed and reached for her pocket diary— had delayed it over three weeks.

It couldn't be that, she thought, not even daring to name the possibility. Not after all these years. But the way she'd felt sick every morning the last week or so, the tingling and swelling of her breasts—

In Aster's mind, the Disneyland figure of Lakshmi reappeared. "I know something you don't know," she seemed to say again, but this time her smile was gentle as well as smug.

I won't mention it, Aster promised herself. Not yet, not until we're home and I've seen Dr. Stewart. It can't be true; but suppose it is?

AFTER THEY HAD CHECKED OUT and had supper, there was still nearly an hour before Clark and Aster had to leave for the airport. For the last time, they strolled down the hotel drive and turned onto Janpath, into a mauvè haze of evening heat and the usual swarm of beggars.

"No baksheesh!" Clark insisted, pushing through them into a shop that sold leather goods which might make good last-minute presents for people in his office. While he leafed through stacks of tooled and dyed wallets, Aster stood at the entrance watching the passing crowd of Indians and foreigners: all ages, all races, all colors.

Suddenly, under a tree at the far edge of the sidewalk, the figure of the goddess Lakshmi appeared: a dark-eyed young woman with matted waist-length black hair and four bare arms. That couldn't be, of course, but it was: one thin dark arm holding her sari together, one outstretched, and two more smaller arms waving above her shoulders; and the same little knowing smile. Aster felt sick and feverish; maybe she was going mad.

The figure of Lakshmi moved, turned; Aster saw that on her back, wrapped in a shawl, its head previously concealed by hers, was a small child, the owner of the second set of arms. They were real, they were beggars—gypsies perhaps.

The beggar woman saw Aster staring; she moved nearer, stretching out one of her four hands. The child looking over her shoulder stared back with its liquid blackberry eyes and gave a faint thin cry. As if in a trance, Aster walked toward them. She opened her handbag, reached in, and pulled out the wad of paper money she had meant to change at the airport.

"Okay, we'd better get back to the hotel," Clark's voice said behind her; and then, "Aster? What are you doing?" But he was too late. The beggar's thin dirty hand had closed over the notes; she turned and hurried off.

Observing their colleague's good fortune, other beggars surged toward Aster, hands clutching her clothing, voices

wailing. But Clark, gripping his wife's arm, pulled her back
into the shop.

"What's going on?" he asked. "How much did you give
that girl?"

"I don't know. Everything," Aster gasped. "She was so
thin. And her baby was crying."

"But darling." Clark put his arm round her. "You had
over fifty dollars in rupees."

"I don't care. I wanted to do something, to make a difference to someone—"

"Well, I guess you did." He laughed. "Fifty dollars, that's
a year's income for a girl like that, maybe more."

"I don't care," Aster said again, her voice shaking.

"Oh, darling." Clark's voice shook too now. "I'm so
sorry."

"I know," Aster said, leaning closer.

"Are you all right?"

"I'm fine. Really." She smiled.

Through the growing dusk, they started back toward the
hotel. Halfway down the block, Aster saw the beggar-girl
again, making her way through the crowd. Her baby
wasn't crying or waving its arms now; it slept heavily
against its mother's back in a fold of ragged shawl.

More than a year's income, Aster thought. Even if what I
think isn't true, something's happened in India. I've made a
difference to that woman and her baby. Maybe I've even
changed their lives.

Do you know that? I've changed your life too! The words
were so loud in her head that Aster was sure she had spoken. But Lakshmi, unhearing, walked on, disappearing into
the noisy, jostling Indian crowd, into the smoky, darkening
city.

Fat People

I NEVER RAN INTO any spooks in sheets, no headless horsemen, haunted mansions, nothing like that. But there was something weird once—

It was a while ago, when Scott went to India on that research grant. The first thing that happened was, I began noticing fat people. I saw them snatching the shrimps and stuffed eggs at parties; I saw them strolling along Cayuga Street with the swaying sailor's gait of the obese, and pawing through the queen-size housecoats in JCPenney. They were buying tubs of popcorn at the flicks, ahead of me in line at the post office and the bank, and pumping self-serve gas into their pickup trucks when I went to the garage.

I didn't pay much attention at first; I figured that since I was dieting I was more aware of people who should be doing the same. My idea was to lose fifteen pounds while Scott was away—twenty if possible, because of what he'd said just before he left.

We were at the county airport on a cold weepy day in March, waiting for Scott's plane and trying to keep up a conversation, repeating things we'd already said. I'd seen Scott off on trips before; but this time he'd be gone over three months. He was saying he wished I were coming, and promising to wire from Delhi and write twice a week, and telling me he loved me and reminding me again to check the oil on the Honda. I said I would, and was there anything else I should do while he was away?

Then the flight was announced and we grabbed each other. But we were both wearing heavy down jackets, and it didn't feel real. It was like two bundles of clothes embracing, I said, all choked up. And Scott said, "Well, there is one thing we could both do while I'm gone, Ellie; we could lose a few pounds." He was kissing my face and I was trying not to break down and howl.

Then Scott was through the X-ray scanner into the boarding lounge, and then he was crossing the wet tarmac with his carry-on bag, getting smaller and smaller, and climbing the steps. It wasn't till I'd gone back to the main waiting room and was standing inside the teary steamed-up window watching his plane shrink and blur into fog that I really registered his last remark.

I drove back to Pine Grove Apartments and dragged off my fat coat and looked at myself in the mirror on the back of the closet door. I knew I was a big girl, at the top of the range for my height, but it had never bothered me before. And as far as I knew it hadn't bothered Scott, who was hefty himself. Maybe when he suggested we lose a few pounds he was just kidding. But it was the last thing I'd hear him say for three months. Or possibly forever, I thought, because India was so far away and full of riots and diseases, and maybe in one of the villages he was going to they wouldn't want to change their thousand-year-old agricultural methods, and they would murder Scott with long wavy decorated knives or serve him curry with thousand-year-old undetectable poisons in it.

I knew it was bad luck to think that way; Scott had said so himself. I looked back at the mirror again, turning sideways. Usually I was pleased by what I saw there, but now I noticed that when I didn't breathe in, my tummy stuck out as far as my breasts.

Maybe I had put on some extra pounds that winter, I thought. Well, it should be pretty easy to take them off. It could be a project, something to do while Scott was gone. I wouldn't write him about it, I'd save it for a surprise when he got back. "Wow, Ellie," he would say, "you look great."

Only it turned out not to be as easy as all that. After two weeks, I weighed exactly the same. One problem was that all our friends kept asking me over and serving meals it would have been a shame to refuse, not to mention rude. And when I didn't have anywhere to go in the evening I started wandering around the apartment and usually ended up wandering into the kitchen and opening the fridge, just for something to do.

It was about then that I began to notice how many fat people there were in town. All sorts and all ages: overweight country-club types easing themselves out of overweight cars; street people shoving rusted grocery carts jammed with bottles and bundles. Fat old men like off-duty Santa Clauses waddling through the shopping mall, fat teenagers with acne, and babies so plump they could hardly get their thumbs into their mouths.

Of course I'd seen types like this before occasionally, but now they seemed to be everywhere. At first I put it down to coincidence, plus having the subject on my mind. It didn't bother me; in a way it was reassuring. When some bulgy high school senior came for an interview at the college, and tried to fit their rear end onto the chair by my desk, I would think as I smiled nicely and asked the standard questions, Well, at least I don't look like that.

My folks knew I was trying to lose weight, and wanted to help, but they only made it worse. Every time I went over to the house for Sunday dinner Dad would ask first thing if I'd heard from Scott. It got to be over three weeks, and I still had to say, "No, nothing since the telegram," and remind them that we'd been warned about how bad the mails were.

Then we'd sit down to the table and Mom would pass my plate, and there'd be this measly thin slice of chicken on it, and a bushel of cooked greens, as if I was in some kind of concentration camp for fatties. The salads all started to have sour low-cal dressing, and there was never anything but fruit for dessert: watery melon, or oranges cut up with a few shreds of dry coconut on top, like little undernourished white worms.

All through the meal Mom and Dad wouldn't mention Scott again, so as not to upset me. There was nothing in the dining room to remind anybody of Scott either, and of course there wasn't any place set for him at the table. It was as if he'd disappeared or maybe had never even existed. By the time dinner was over I'd be so low in my mind I'd have to stop on the way home for a pint of chocolate marshmallow.

I'd hang up my coat and turn on the television and measure out exactly half a cup of ice cream, 105 calories, less than a bagel. I'd put the rest in the freezer and feel virtuous. But when the next commercial came on I'd open the freezer and have a few more spoonfuls. And then the whole process would repeat, like a commercial, until the carton was scraped clean down to the wax.

It got to be four weeks since Scott had left, and I still didn't weigh any less, even when I shifted my feet on the scale to make the needle wobble downward. I'd never tried to lose weight before; I'd always thought it was ridiculous the way some people went into agonies over diets. I'd even been kind of shocked when one of my married friends made more fuss about taking a second slice of peach pie than she did about taking a lover. Displaced guilt, I used to think.

Now I was as hysterical about food as any of them. I brooded all afternoon over a fudge brownie I hadn't had for lunch; and if I broke down and ordered one I made up excuses for hours afterward. I didn't promise Scott I'd lose weight, I would tell myself, or It's not fair asking someone to give up both food and love at the same time.

I started to read all the articles on losing weight that I used to skip before, and I took books out of the library. Over the next couple of weeks I tried one crazy diet after another: no-carbohydrate, no-fat, grapefruit and corn-flakes, chipped beef and bananas and skim milk. Only I couldn't stick with any of them. Things went wrong at night when I started thinking about how I'd written nine letters to Scott and hadn't got one back. I'd lie in bed asking myself where the hell was he, what was he doing now? And pretty soon I'd feel hungry, starving.

Another thing I kept asking myself, especially when I chewed through some dried-out salad or shook Sweet 'n Low into my coffee, was what Scott, assuming he was still alive, was eating over there on the other side of the world. If he wasn't on a diet, what was the point? I would think, watching my hand reach out for the blue-cheese dressing or the half-and-half. He hadn't meant it seriously, I'd tell myself.

But suppose he had meant it? Suppose Scott was becoming slimmer and trimmer every day; what would he think if he knew I hadn't lost a pound in nearly five weeks?

Trying to do it on my own wasn't working. I needed support, and I thought I knew where to find it. There was a young woman in the Admissions Office called Dale. She was only a couple of years older than me, maybe twenty-six, but in two months she'd just about reorganized our files, and she obviously had her life under control. She was a brunette, with a narrow neat little figure and a narrow neat little poodle face; you got the feeling her hair wouldn't dare get itself mussed up, and she'd never weigh one ounce more than she chose to.

I figured that Dale would have ideas about my problem, because she was always talking about interesting new diets. And whenever some really heavy person came in she'd make a yapping noise under her breath and remark later how awful it was for people to let themselves go physically. "Heaven knows how that hippopotamus is going to fulfill his athletic requirement," she would say, or "That girl's mother ought to be in a circus; she hardly looked human." And I'd think, Do I look human to Dale?

So one day when we were alone in the washroom I let on that I was trying to lose some weight. Dale lit up like a fluorescent tube. "Yes, I think that's a good idea, Ellie," she said, looking from herself to me, poodle to hippo, in the mirror over the basins. "And I'd like to help you, okay?"

"Okay, thanks," I said. I didn't have any idea what I was getting into.

On our way back to the office, Dale explained to me that being overweight was a career handicap. It was a known fact that heavy people didn't get ahead as fast in business. Besides, fat was low-class: the Duchess of Windsor had said you could never be too rich or too thin. When I told her there wasn't much danger of my ever being either one, Dale didn't laugh. She printed her Duchess of Windsor line out in computer-graphic caps, and fastened it on the side of my filing cabinet with two pineapple magnets.

The next thing Dale did was persuade me to see a doctor to make sure I was healthy, the way they tell you to do in the diet books. Then she started organizing my life. She got me enrolled in an aerobics class, and set up a schedule for me to jog every day after work, regardless of the weather. Then she invited herself over to my apartment and cleaned out the cupboards and icebox. Bags of pretzels and fritos, butter and cream cheese and cold cuts, a loaf of cinnamon-raisin bread, most of a pound of Jones bacon— Dale packed everything up, and we hauled it down to the local soup kitchen. I kind of panicked when I saw all that lovely food disappearing, but I was hopeful too.

The next day Dale brought in a calorie counter and planned my meals for a week in advance. She kept a chart, and every day she'd ask how much I'd weighed that morning and write it down.

Only the scale still stuck at the same number. If there was nothing in the apartment, there was always plenty in the grocery. I'd go in for celery and cottage cheese and Ry-Krisp, but when I was pushing the cart down the last aisle it was as if the packages of cookies on the shelves were crying out to me, especially the chocolate-covered grahams and the Mallomars. I could almost hear them squeaking inside their cellophane wrappers, in these little high sugary voices: "Ellie, Ellie! Here we are, Ellie!"

When I confessed to falling off my diet, Dale didn't lose her cool. "Never mind, Ellie, that's all right," she said. "I know what we'll do. From now on, don't you go near a supermarket alone. I'll shop with you twice a week on the way home."

So the next day she did. But as soon as she got a little ahead of me in the bakery section, I began drifting toward a tray of apricot croissants. Dale looked round and shook her poodle curls and said, "Naughty, naughty"—which kind of made me feel crazy, because I hadn't done anything naughty yet—and then she grabbed my arm and pulled me along fast.

There'd been several fat people in the A & P that day, the

way there always were lately. When we were in line at the checkout with a load of groceries only a rabbit could love, I noticed one of them, a really heavy blonde girl about my own age, leaving the next register. Her cart was full, and a couple of plump bakery boxes, a carton of potato chips, and a giant bottle of Coke were bulging out of the brown-paper bags. As she came past the fat girl picked up a package of Hershey bars and tore it open, and half-smiled in my direction as if she were saying, "Come on, Ellie, have one."

I looked round at Dale, figuring she would make some negative comment, but she didn't. Maybe she hadn't seen the fat girl yet. The funny thing was, when I looked back I didn't see her either; she must have been in a big rush to get home. And she was going to have a really good time when she got there, too, I thought.

Another week dragged by full of carrots and diet soda and frozen Weight Watchers dinners, and no news from Scott. My diet wasn't making much progress either. I'd take a couple of pounds off, but then I'd go out to dinner or a party and put three or four back on. Instead of losing I was gaining.

I was still seeing fat people too, more and more of them. I tried to convince myself it was just because they weren't disguised inside winter clothes any longer. The only problem was, the people I was seeing weren't just heavy, they were gross.

The first time I knew for sure that something strange was going on was one day when I was in the shopping plaza downtown, sitting on the edge of a planter full of sticky purple petunias and listening to a band concert instead of eating lunch, which had been Dale's idea naturally. I was feeling kind of dizzy and sick, and when I touched my head it seemed to vibrate, as if it wasn't attached to my body too well.

Then I happened to glance across the plaza, and through

the window of the Home Bakery I saw two middle-aged women, both of them bulging out of flowered blouses and slacks as if they'd been blown up too full. I couldn't make out their faces well because of the way the light shimmered and slid on the shop window; but I could see that one of them was looking straight at me and pointing to a tray of strawberry tarts: big ones with thick ruby glaze and scallops of whipped cream. It was as if she was saying, "Come and get it, Ellie."

Without even intending to I stood up and started to push through the crowd. But when I reached the bakery there weren't any fat women, and I hadn't seen them leave either. There'd been a moment when I was blocked by a twin stroller; but it still didn't make sense, unless maybe the fat women hadn't really been there. Suddenly I started feeling sick to my stomach. I didn't want a strawberry tart anymore; I just wanted to go somewhere and lie down, only I was due back in the Admissions Office.

When I got there I said to Dale, making my voice casual, "You know something funny, I keep seeing all these really fat people around lately."

"There are a lot of them around, Ellie," Dale said. "Americans are terribly overweight."

"But I'm seeing more. I mean, lots more than I ever did before. I mean, do you think that's weird?"

"You're just noticing them more," Dale said, stapling forms together bang-bang. "Most people block out unpleasant sights of that sort. They don't see the disgusting rubbish in the streets, or the way the walls are peeling right in this office." She pointed with her head to a corner above the swing doors, where the cream-colored paint was swollen into bubbles and flaking away; I hadn't noticed it before. Somehow that made me feel better.

"I guess you could be right," I said. I knew that Dale was getting impatient with me. She'd stopped keeping my weight chart, and when we went shopping now she read the labels on things aloud in a cross way, as if she suspected I was cheating on my diet and had a package of shortbread or a box of raisins hidden away at home, which was sometimes true.

It was around that time that eating and sex started to get mixed up in my mind. Sometimes at night I still woke up hot and tense and longing for Scott; but more often I got excited about food. I read articles on cooking and restaurants in a greedy lingering way, and had fantasies about veal paprika with sour cream and baby onions, or lemon meringue pie. Once after I'd suddenly gone up to a pushcart and bought a giant hot dog with ketchup and relish I heard myself saying half aloud, "I just had to have it." And that reminded me of the way men talked in tough-guy thrillers. "I had to have her," they always said, and they would speak of some woman as if she was a rich dessert and call her a dish or a cupcake and describe parts of her as melons or buns. Scott isn't really a macho type, but he's always liked thrillers; he says they relax him on trips. And when he got on the plane that awful day he'd had one with him.

He'd been gone over six weeks by then, and no news since the telegram from Delhi. Either something really terrible had happened to him or he deliberately wasn't writing. Maybe while I was cheating on my diet, Scott was cheating on me, I thought. Maybe he'd found some Indian cupcake to relax him. As soon as I had that idea I tried to shove it out of my head, but it kept oozing back.

Then one sunny afternoon early in June I came home from work and opened the mailbox, and there among the bills and circulars was a postcard from Scott. There wasn't any apology for not writing, just a couple of lines about a beautiful temple he'd visited, and a scrawled "love and kisses." On the other side was a picture of a sexy overdecorated Indian woman and a person or god with the head of an elephant, both of them wearing smug smiles.

As I looked at that postcard something kind of exploded inside me. For weeks I'd been telling myself and everyone, "If only I knew Scott was all right, I'd feel fine." Now I knew he was all right, but what I felt was a big rush of suspicion and fury.

Pictures from the coffee-table books on India Scott had borrowed from the library crowded into my mind. I saw sleek prune-eyed exotic beauties draped in shiny silk and jewels, looking at me with hard sly expressions; and plump nearly naked blue gods with bedroom eyes; and close-ups of temple sculptures in pockmarked stone showing one thousand and one positions for sexual intercourse. The idea came to me that at that exact moment Scott was making out in one thousand different positions with some woman who had an elephant's head or was completely blue. I knew that was crazy, but still he had to be doing something he didn't want to tell me about and was ashamed of, or he would have written.

I didn't go on upstairs to the apartment. Instead I got back into the car, not knowing where I was going till the Honda parked of its own volition in front of a gourmet shop and cafe that I hadn't been near for weeks. There were five other customers there, which wasn't unusual at that time of day. The unusual thing was, all of them were fat; and not just overweight: humongously huge. All of them looked at me in a friendly way when I came in, as if maybe they knew me and had something to tell me.

For a moment I couldn't move. I just stood there stuck to the indoor-outdoor carpeting and wondered if I was going out of my mind. Five out of five; it wasn't reasonable, but there they were, or anyhow I was seeing them.

The fat people knew about Scott, I thought. They'd known all along. That was what they'd been trying to say to me when they smiled and held up cones or candy bars: "Come on, honey, why should you deny yourself? You can bet your life Scott isn't."

A huge guy with a grizzly-bear beard left the counter, giving me a big smile, and I placed my order. A pound of assorted butter cookies, a loaf of cinnamon bread, and a date-walnut coffee ring with white sugar icing. As soon as I got into the car I tore open the box and broke off a piece of the coffee ring, and it was fantastic: the sweet flaky yellow pastry, and the sugar-glazed walnuts; a lot better than sex with Scott, I told myself.

For the next four days I pigged out. I finished the cookies and coffee ring that same evening, and on Friday afternoon I sneaked over to the grocery without telling Dale and bought everything I'd dreamt about for weeks: bacon and sausages and sliced Virginia ham, butter and sour cream and baking potatoes, pretzels and barbecue potato chips and frozen french fries. And that was just the beginning.

When I went in to work Monday morning with a box of assorted jelly doughnuts I let Dale know I was off my diet for good. Dale tried to shove me back on. It didn't really matter about the weekend binge, she yipped. If I skipped lunch all week and cut way down on dinner and jogged two miles a day I'd be back on track.

"I don't want to be on track," I told her. "Eight weeks Scott has been gone, and all I've had from him is one disgusting postcard."

Dale looked pained and started talking about self-respect and self-image, but I wasn't having any. "Leave me alone, please," I said. "I know what I'm doing."

TWO DAYS and a lot of pork chops and baked potatoes and chicken salad and chocolate almond bark and cherry pie later, I walked into my building, steadied a bag of high-calorie groceries against my hip, and opened the mailbox.

Jesus, I practically dropped the bag. The galvanized-metal slot was crammed with fat white and flimsy blue air-mail letters from India. Most of them looked as if they'd been opened and read and crumpled up and walked on, and they were covered with stamps and cancellations.

An hour later, sitting on my sofa surrounded by two months' worth of Scott's letters, I faced facts. He was dieting: his second letter said so, mentioning that he didn't want to look overfed when he walked through a village full of hungry people. All right. I had three weeks, which meant —I went into the bathroom and dragged out the scale from the bottom of the cupboard where I'd shoved it on Friday— Which meant, oh God, I'd have to lose over two pounds a week just to get back to where I was when Scott left.

It was an awful three weeks. I had cereal and skim milk and fruit for breakfast and lunch, to get through work, but otherwise I didn't eat anything much. Pretty soon I was blurred and headachy most of the time, in spite of all the vitamins and minerals I was scarfing down, and too tired to exercise. And I was still behind schedule on losing weight.

What made it worse was the fat people. I was seeing them again everywhere, only now they didn't look happy or friendly. "You're making a big mistake, Ellie," they seemed to be telling me at first. Then they began to get angry and disgusted. "Sure, he wrote you, stupid," their expressions said. "That doesn't prove he's not helping himself to some Indian dish right this minute."

I quit going out after work; I didn't have the energy. Mostly I just stayed home drinking diet soda and rereading Scott's letters, kind of to prove to myself that he existed, I guess, because there hadn't been any more. Then I'd watch a little television and go to bed early, hoping to forget about food for a while. But for the first time in my life I was having insomnia, jolting awake in the small hours and lying there starving.

The day Scott was due back, I woke up about 4 A.M. and couldn't doze off again even with Valium. For what seemed like hours I thrashed around in bed. Finally I got up and opened a can of diet soda and switched on the TV. Only now, on all the channels that were still broadcasting, everybody was overweight: the third-string newscasters, the punk MTV singers, the comics in an old black-and-white film. On the weather channel I could tell that the girl was hiding thighs like hams under the pleated skirt she kept swishing around as she pointed out the tornado areas. Then the picture changed and a soft plump guy smiled from between chipmunk cheeks and told me that airports were fogged in all over Europe and Scott would never get home.

I turned off the television, dragged on some jeans and a T-shirt, and went out. It was a warm June night full of noises: other tenants' air conditioners and fans, traffic out on the highway; and planes overhead. There was a hard wind blowing, which made me feel kind of dizzy and slapped about, and it was that uneasy time just before dawn when you start to see shapes but can't make out colors. The sky was a pale sick lemon, but everything else was lumps of blurred grey.

Pine Grove Apartments is surrounded on three sides by an access road, and I'd just turned the corner and was starting toward the dead end. That was when I saw them, way down by the trees. There was a huge sexless person with long stringy hair waving its arms and walking slowly toward me out of the woods, and behind it came more angry fat grey people, and then more and more.

I wanted to run, but I knew somehow that if I turned round the fat people would rush after me the way kids do when you play Giant Steps, and they would catch me and, God, I didn't know what. So I just backed up slowly step by step toward the corner of the building, breathing in shallow gasps.

They kept coming out of the woods in the half-light, more and more, maybe ten or twenty or fifty, I didn't know. I thought I recognized the women from the bakery, and the big guy with the beard— And then I realized I could hear them too, kind of mumbling and wailing. I couldn't take it anymore. I turned and raced for home, stumbling over the potholes in the drive.

Well, somehow I made it to the apartment, and slammed the door and double-locked it and put on the chain, and leaned up against the wall panting and gulping. For what seemed like hours I stood there, listening to the sounds of the fat people coming after me, crowding up the stairs, all grey and blubbery, and roaring and sobbing and sliding and thumping against the walls and door.

Then the noises started to change. Gradually they turned into the wind in the concrete stairwell and the air conditioner downstairs and the six-thirty plane to New York flying over the complex and a dog barking somewhere. It was light out now, nearly seven o'clock. I unbolted my door, keeping the chain on, and eased it open a slow inch. The hall was empty.

I still felt completely exhausted and crazy, but I got myself dressed somehow and choked down some coffee and left for work. On the way I took a detour in the Honda round the corner of the building. At first I was afraid to look, even though I was safe inside the locked car. At the edge of the woods where the mob of fat people had been there was nothing but some big old spirea bushes blowing and tossing about.

THAT EVENING Scott came home, ten pounds overweight. A couple of days later, when he was talking about his trip, he said that Indian food was great, especially the sweets, but the women were hard to talk to and not all that good-looking.

"A lot of Indians are heavy too, you know," he told me.

"Really?" I asked. I wondered if Scott had had some spooky experience like mine, which I still hadn't mentioned: I didn't want him to think I was going to crack up whenever he left town.

"It's a sign of prosperity, actually. You notice them especially in the cities, much more than in this country. I mean, you don't see many fat people around here, for instance, do you?"

"No," I agreed, cutting us both another slice of pineapple upside-down cake. "Not lately, anyhow."

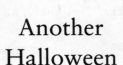

Another
Halloween

YOU'VE GOT TO ADMIT there's something uncomfortable about Halloween as a holiday. I mean, what are we celebrating? Not the American Revolution, or the family, or God, or the New Year, nothing like that. Nothing respectable. Instead of flags or holly or colored lights, the streets are full of weird-looking dwarfish creatures, monsters and witches and animals running on their hind legs. You might say, Oh, they're only our kids, and other people's kids. But how do you know for sure?

In ancient Rome, where the whole thing started according to what I've read, they called it the Day of the Dead. That was who came back every year and they didn't come back in good shape or in a good mood. The dead were disoriented and destructive, like people in a late stage of Alzheimer's. They slid out of their tombs at sunset and drifted through town in their trailing, rotted grave clothes, gabbling unintelligibly in Latin. It's in Shakespeare: "the

sheeted dead/Did squeak and gibber in the Roman streets."
People left out saucers of food and drink, and barricaded
themselves in their houses, which was probably the smart
thing to do.

I don't care much for Halloween, not since what happened to a woman I knew called Marguerite Robbins. She
lived next door to us in Corinth when our children were
small, in one of a block of clunky frame houses, too close
together. They were roomy inside though, with big old
kitchens and deep front porches. I was really close to a
couple of the other young mothers on the block; they were
like family, maybe better than family.

It wasn't that way with Marguerite. But her Jamie was
our Joel's age, and they were best friends, so we met practically every day. We got on well enough; but I always felt
kind of overgrown and clumsy around her; she was so dain-
tily pretty: pale blonde, with a round baby face and short-
fingered hands like an expensive doll. Her nails were a
matched set of tiny perfect polished shells. She wore rubber
gloves for housework, and makeup even at breakfast: pow-
der-pink lipstick and powder-blue eye shadow.

Also she made me feel noisy. She had the sort of cool
manners that always make me think of words like *pleasant*
and *cordial*. She never had much to say, or raised her voice,
and she didn't like it when somebody else did. If I blew my
top because Joel'd wet the bed again, or the washer
wouldn't drain, she would murmur, "Oh, that's too bad,"
and literally move back, as if a wave full of dirty seaweed
had slopped too close to her on a beach.

Anyhow. The weird stuff started the Robbinses' first Halloween, a month or so after they moved in. All the older
kids on the block had gone out trick-and-treating, but Jamie and Joel were still too small. Marguerite's husband had
a meeting and she asked if I'd like to keep her company.
From the sound of her voice I knew she was imagining

teenage hooligans who would smash her windows or squirt red paint over her when she opened the door. I told her nothing like that ever happened in our neighborhood, but she didn't sound convinced.

So I asked Fred to hold the fort and went over to Marguerite's maple-and-chintz Early American sitting room, which always reminded me of our dentist's office. She had a big basket of polished Golden Delicious apples and little boxes of raisins on the table by the door. Not what I would have chosen; let's face it, kids want candy.

At first there were so many trick-and-treaters we hardly had time to drink our coffee, but then things slowed down and I began to consider going home.

Then the bell rang again. I heaved myself up in case it might be someone I knew, though I was eight months pregnant and felt like a bathtub on wheels. There were four or five kids: a cute lady pirate, a Mickey Mouse, and a couple of tramps with burnt-cork mustaches and eyebrows, but nobody I recognized.

Marguerite handed out the health food and shut the door, and then she turned and asked in a wound-up voice, "Ruthie, who was that child in the rabbit costume?"

I hadn't noticed any, I said.

"In back of the others. She was wearing one of those bunny sleepers with feet, and a white mask."

I shook my head.

"You must have seen her," Marguerite insisted. "About five years old, and she had an old wrinkled white pillow-case for a bag."

"Nope; I'm sorry."

Marguerite gave me a look that said I was stupid and unobservant. Then she went back to the sitting room and poured herself more coffee without offering me any, which was really unusual for her.

"It's just—" she said, holding her cup in both doll's

hands, not looking at me but out the window at the light from her jack-o'-lantern wavering on the porch railings. "You see, when I was a child— The little sister of a girl I knew was hit by a car on Halloween, and she was wearing a costume like that. So it rather upset me."

"Well, hell, of course," I agreed. "What an awful thing to happen!"

"I wasn't involved, actually," said Marguerite. "I knew her by sight, that was all. But it *was* rather awful. More coffee?"

"No thanks." I was glowing with sympathy like an electric heater. "It's always so damn scary when a child gets hurt, even if you hardly know them. Last summer this little boy was visiting across the street, and he fell off his tricycle and cut his head open. While I was running toward him I felt this absolute panic— I should have known it couldn't be that bad, because he'd got right up again, but he was screaming so loud, and his face was covered in blood, though in the end he only had to have two stitches. I could hardly breathe, I was sort of—"

"Yes, I remember you telling me," Marguerite interrupted.

"Oh, did I? Sorry." I shut up.

"Glen should be home soon," she added, and then she politely swallowed a yawn: she didn't open her pretty rose-pink mouth, but her whole face got longer in that unmistakable way. So I took the hint and left.

WELL, TIME PASSED, and I almost forgot the whole business. I saw Marguerite often because of the kids, but I hadn't got to like her much better. Maybe it was her nicey-nice manners, or her attitude toward local projects. You know how it is, somebody's always trying to organize sales of Girl Scout cookies or soliciting for the Heart Fund, or asking you to go door-to-door with a petition to save wild-life. Most of us usually went along, but not Marguerite.

What really put me off was the cool, composed way she always refused. For instance, one time Joel and Jamie's day-care center was holding a raffle to fund a new climbing frame, and I asked Marguerite to take a couple of tickets. They were only a dollar each, and you could win a week-end in New York or a heap of other prizes. If it had been me who couldn't come up with two bucks I would have fallen all over myself apologizing. Marguerite just said po-litely, "Oh, no thank you, Ruthie," as if I'd offered her a stale doughnut.

WHEN HALLOWEEN CAME ROUND again Joel and Ja-mie were four, old enough for trick-and-treating, and I vol-unteered to take them. Jamie was a clown, and Joel had got it into his head to be Little Bear; I had to go to three stores to find the fake fur, but I have to say he looked pretty damn cute. Marguerite didn't come with us: her husband was home, but he had a report to write and couldn't be dis-turbed, or so she said.

Well, next morning just after Joel and Jamie had left for day care there was a knock at the back door, and it was Marguerite. Which was odd to start with, because she al-ways phoned first to see if it was a "good time" to come over.

She looked terrible. Her pink lipstick was on crooked, and her flowered blouse was buttoned wrong, so that one side of its Peter Pan collar seemed about to take off.

"Well, hi. Come on in," I said.

Marguerite took half a step forward; then she just stood in a sort of huddle by the door. "I wanted to thank you again," she said. "For taking Jamie out last night. He really," she started again, and stopped dead.

"That's okay, it was fun. He's a good kid," I said, which

was true. "Here, have some coffee." I pulled out a chair and she sat down kind of uneven, on one edge of it.

Then the kettle began boiling and whistling, and Fred walked into the room behind her and called out "Rabbit!" for good luck because it was the first day of the month. That's a family tradition, dating back to when we met. I hadn't heard of the custom then, and when I woke up in Fred's bedroom for the first time I saw him standing by the open window in his bathrobe and he called, "Rabbit!" and I said, "Oh, where?" and I jumped up naked and ran to look out, and I was practically face-to-face and chest to chest with two guys playing Frisbee. I hadn't noticed the night before that his apartment building was on a slope, the way most everything is in Corinth.

Anyhow. My startle reaction that day in Fred's room wasn't a patch on Marguerite's. She looked as if she were going to throw up, and her mug slipped and splashed the table with coffee.

"I'm terribly sorry," she squeaked, and then she didn't utter a word until Fred had chugged down his orange juice and gone out for his run.

Then she leaned forward and said in a kind of loud whisper, "I saw her again, Ruthie. That same little girl who came to the house last year."

"Little girl?" I said. Then I remembered. "You mean the one in the bunny costume, that reminded you of some kid you once knew."

"Yes, did you see her?"

"No, sorry. But of course we weren't out long."

"She came again." Marguerite announced this as if it were some really bad world news.

"Oh yeah?" I was skeptical. "Are you sure it was the same one? I mean, hell, there must have been lots of little kids out last night in those bunny sleepers. Besides, you know most children won't wear the same costume two years running. You remember that fairy getup with the gauze wings Josie made for Mary Lou last year, a size too large so she could use it again, only now Mary Lou doesn't believe in fairies, she had to be a space pilot—" Then I happened to look at Marguerite's face and shut up.

"It was the same little girl," she said. She was tormenting the paper napkin I'd given her, twisting it round and round. "With that same old pillowcase. And the left ear of the rabbit mask bent sideways, and her eyes looking at me through the holes."

"Maybe you just thought it was her," I suggested. It had occurred to me that when Marguerite had seen that accident she had got a childhood trauma, and since then anybody in a bunny sleeper was a reminder. "Because of that kid you knew who got hit by a car."

"Killed," Marguerite said. "She was killed." She wrung the neck of the paper napkin. "I was there."

That wasn't what you told me last year, I started to say, but I made an effort and swallowed it.

"I wasn't really involved, of course. I was simply out trick-or-treating with her older sister," Marguerite went on finally. "My friend's mother made her take Kelly with us. Only round the block, and then she was supposed to go home, but she wouldn't. Annie gave her a push up the front walk, but she just stood there, whining that it wasn't fair, because we were going to get more candy.

"We ignored her, but Kelly started following us down the street. She kept calling, 'Wait for me, wait for me!' and we shouted back, 'Go on home, you stupid baby!'

"Finally we started running to get away from her. We got to the corner and ran across North Avenue, and Kelly ran after us. Only she couldn't run very fast, or see very well through the rabbit mask, and an old lady in a Buick came around the corner and hit her."

"Oh, God," I said. "And you saw it happen? That's terrible."

"I didn't actually see the car hit her. But I heard it: first this high shriek, that was the brakes, and then somebody screaming. Only it wasn't Kelly screaming, it was the old lady driver. Kelly was just lying by the curb under the streetlight, with her rabbit face turned sideways, not moving. Except her pillowcase was open, and Tootsie Rolls and candy corn were rolling all over the pavement."

"God," I said. "Well, no wonder you freak out when somebody shouts 'Rabbit!' After my aunt left the space heater on and her summer cottage practically burned down with her in it, she said that whenever she smelled wood smoke, for the next twenty years—" I stopped myself. "Hey, I'm sorry. I mean, of course it upset you."

"It didn't really upset me," Marguerite said. "After all, I wasn't responsible. Naturally I was disturbed at the time, but I got over it." She took a breath and smiled as if her teeth hurt.

"Mm," I said, making a big effort not to contradict her. "Well, I guess it was worse for the family."

"Oh, yes. It more or less ruined their lives, as a matter of fact."

"Really."

"And the driver's, too. She was cleared in court, but she sold the Buick and gave up her license, because she still felt guilty, even though it wasn't anybody's fault. Then she tried to give Kelly's family quite a lot of money, but they were too angry to accept it."

"Really?" I said, though afterward when I thought about it I wasn't so surprised.

"Yes; that was odd. But about ten years later she died and left it to them anyway. Only by that time Kelly's parents were divorced and her sister was in a drug treatment center. And naturally the old lady's own relatives didn't care for it at all. They tried to break the will." Marguerite smiled again; it was her normal little sweet smile now.

"What a depressing story," I said.

"Yes, it is, rather," agreed Marguerite. She seemed quite recovered except for her blouse, which was still buttoned wrong. "Well, I'd better get back. Thank you for the coffee."

After she left I sat there for a while. It had finally dawned on me that what she thought she kept seeing on Halloween was the ghost of the little girl who'd been killed. Then I had an idea. I thought that if I could find the actual kid who'd been wearing that bunny costume the night before, Marguerite would get over her delusion.

During the next few days I asked almost everyone on the block, only it turned out nobody had seen any bunny rabbits. I finally decided the kid must have come in a car, the way you heard people from the projects do sometimes. They get their children dressed up and take them to some part of town where they can collect expensive candy, and maybe even money. Of course the right part of Corinth for that was on the other side of the campus, but maybe whoever was driving the car didn't realize it till their kids had been to Marguerite's house on the corner and collected her depressing apples and raisins.

AFTER THAT I forgot the whole thing for a while. I had a one-year-old and a four-year-old and I was trying to hold down a part-time job and half-asleep on my feet most of the time. Marguerite seemed to be okay again, only I was getting kind of tired of her. We'd been living next door for over two years, but after that once she would never talk about anything personal. If you asked who she liked in the local elections, or if she'd been happy in kindergarten, she'd just give you that cool polite little smile and say, "I haven't thought about it," or "I really can't remember." And I'd begun to notice that she always did a little bit less than her share of driving and watching the kids, something Fred and other people had mentioned a while back.

Most of the other mothers on the block were seriously fed up with Marguerite by this time, especially Josie, my best pal across the street, who had never forgiven her for refusing to help campaign against the waste-disposal plant. Marguerite had remarked that after all, by the time the plant was built most of us would probably have moved away. If you knew Josie, you'd know that was about the worst excuse anybody could have thought of.

What I didn't like most of all was that Josie and the rest of them kind of acted as if I was responsible for Marguerite. "Do you want to know what your friend has done now?" somebody would say, for instance. "She's not my friend," I'd want to answer, but instead I'd start making up excuses for Marguerite, blaming her husband, or the migraine headaches she used to have.

Anyhow, it got to be another Halloween—our last one in Corinth, but we didn't know that then. Joel and Jamie were five, still too young to go out on their own. It was Marguerite's turn to take them, and for once her husband had agreed to give away the treats. She asked if I wanted to come along, and I said okay. I knew Joel would like it, and besides I thought maybe Marguerite was nervous about being out on her own because of her delusion about the rabbit.

It was an unpleasant night: cold and wet, with rain leaking down through the bare trees, and drifts of greenish-grey fog rising from the pavement. Joel was got up as a red dinosaur—what a job that had been—and Jamie was some kind of space monster. They both thought they were pretty fierce; they kept growling at everyone we met, and they'd refused to wear their slickers. Also they didn't want us to come to the door with them—we had to wait on the path out of the light, under our umbrellas.

When we were halfway around the block and on our way home I happened to look down the street and saw a bunch of kids crossing the road, maybe thirty feet away. The smallest one, trailing behind the rest, was wearing a bunny sleeper.

That was when I made my first bad mistake. I said to Marguerite, "Hey, look, there's a kid in a rabbit costume, like the one you saw last year."

She went all white and funny. "Where?" she squeaked, and stared round like someone who hears an explosion and doesn't know what direction it came from.

I pointed down the street. The little kid had stopped at the far corner and was looking back at us. She gave a kind of wave, or maybe she was just trying to get a better grip on the pillowcase she was dragging, and then she went on, running to catch up to the others.

"I've got to see— Would you mind? I'll be right back," Marguerite said.

"Sure, that's okay," I agreed. I figured Marguerite would find out who the kid was, and get over being knocked sideways every time she saw a rabbit.

Marguerite didn't even say thanks. She was already hurrying down the wet sidewalk: running a few steps in the high heels she always wore, then walking a few, then running again.

"Wait for me!" she called. But the rabbit was only a white blob now down at the end of the next block, and it didn't stop; maybe it hadn't even heard.

For a moment I just stood there, even though Joel and Jamie were already pulling at me, wanting to go on to the next house. I could see Marguerite's pale raincoat and paler hair shine and dim as she moved through the cones of misty brightness under the street lamps, getting smaller and farther away. Unloading your job on me again, was what I thought. Then she turned a corner, and that was the last I saw of her.

We finished the block, and Marguerite still wasn't back. I took Jamie home and told Glen his wife had gone to speak to some child she thought she knew, and he said, "Oh, okay."

But later at our house, when Joel was dumping his candy onto the kitchen table, I had the idea that maybe I should go out again and look for Marguerite. I even started to put on my raincoat.

If it had been one of my real friends I would've gone without thinking. But instead I paused and said to myself, What's the point? Whether or not she's caught up with the kid in the bunny costume, she has to be back soon. And if you do find her she'll give you that polite look that is her specialty. What are you doing here, why are you sticking your nose into my business? that look will say, the way it so often has.

I don't think that way anymore. Now I believe women have to take responsibility for other women, even ones they don't much like. And I think that if I'd gone after Marguerite maybe I would have been in time.

NONE OF US heard the crash. It was four long blocks off anyhow, on the main road. The guy who hit her claimed Marguerite just rushed out in front of his old Buick convertible, but nobody believed him because he already had two convictions for DWI, so he got six months and lost his license. I felt a little sorry for him, but I didn't say anything.

I think about it sometimes. I tell myself that Corinth was probably full of bunny sleepers that night, and that lots of people give their kids old pillowcases to collect candy in. I try to believe I just imagined that the rabbit's mask had one ear bent down; or that even if it did, it wouldn't be anything to get into a state about.

But that's not the worst. The worst is that sometimes I'm convinced she's still out there, and I'll see her again. Not the little girl in the bunny costume: Marguerite. I can't get rid of the idea that some Halloween night when I look out past the little witches and clowns and spacemen on our porch, she'll be there too: standing halfway down the path in her pale raincoat under a bat-black umbrella, waiting for me.

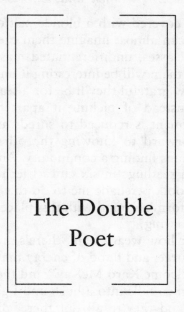

The Double Poet

SEPTEMBER

AFTER OVER TWO WEEKS, I'm still unsettled, uneasy here. I agreed to be this year's Visiting Poet largely because the photographs in the college catalogue showed a landscape as lovely and transcendent as my enchanted Cape Cod pond. They lied: I'm awash in shopping malls and Lego-brick dormitories, boxed into a cardboard box apartment complex. I believe I *have* an apartment complex— have had one since I arrived. Claustrophobia: three cramped lowering rooms. Paranoia: the kitchenette sink's chronic water-torture drip. Hallucinations: ugly voices and uglier music seeping from adjoining apartments as a nearly visible sludge. No wonder I'm finding it difficult to write.

Yet the countryside is handsome: it lacks delicacy and subtlety but has a sweep, a fecundity— Rounded fields like sleeping beasts, covered with a blonde pelt of ripening hay and corn. One can almost imagine them breathing.

I've met my classes, undifferentiated masses as yet, but perhaps among them will be interesting if unformed beings. And I know how grateful they'll be for a teacher who celebrates poetry instead of picking it apart till a seamless, shimmering garment is reduced to shreds and tatters. Am also looking forward to knowing the other writers who teach here, perhaps finding a community. And beginning to regret the seven readings in six cities I let my new lecture agent, Bryan Wood, persuade me to do this year. Will they strain my slow-forming bond with this place, be physically, emotionally wearying?

Yet no matter how weary I am, there's always the thrilling gathering, surge, and flood of energy that comes when I hear "Please welcome Karo McKay" and the soft clatter of applause rises, then falls into a hush and I glide forward in my long dress and they're all out there, dim rapt flower faces turned to the light—waiting, wanting, needing what I bring them.

Because somehow I validate their private experience—especially their experience of the sensual world. My words, my voice somehow allow them to see, hear, touch, smell, feel; to, as one used to put it, Be Here Now—not shut themselves off from life with sad self-conscious hesitation.

As even I once used to. How long ago they seem now, my first awkward, fearful readings before tiny audiences—back when I was still only Carrie Martin. When I knew nothing, expected no reward, hardly dared dream of what was to come. In dusty black beatnik outfit of leotard and dance skirt, I stumbled through a shaking sheaf of papers. I didn't even know enough to memorize my poems, didn't know how to project them, project my voice, project myself.

I didn't yet realize that a poet is, must be, both creator and performer. Those whose work, however deeply felt or original, is essentially addressed only to the printed page are only half-poets. They won't or can't let themselves be truly, vividly *heard,* they read flatly, badly, rarely, sometimes not at all. Their poems are half-poems.

Bryan W has been most helpful, not only in asking for higher fees, which one can't gracefully do oneself, but in arranging all the details. Assuring that I shall never be roused till nine, will always have an hour alone to rest and recharge after I arrive, and iced Perrier on the podium instead of tap water. I anticipated difficulty over these requests, but Bryan assures me that in fact his clients like to think that writers have special needs, are more sensitive to their environment. Which I suppose we are.

I believe I'll wear the midnight-blue cape again—it has such a fine sweep and flow—and alternate the white lace dress and the new sea-green silk that the interviewer in Washington said made me look like a classical sibyl. Must get shoes to go with it—a darker green silk perhaps? Renew the little V prescription, I've used so many during this wretched move. And redo my tape: the ocean sounds should fade more gradually at the end, and I need something to go with "Distant Pleasures"—more Satie? Bird song?

FOUR WEEKS NOW. Heavy, hot weather, and I am tiring of the heavy, hot inland landscape. Even out in the countryside I feel confined by the stale weight of the air, the ponderous laden trees and dense shrubbery; by the sense of being a hundred miles from my shining, ever-changing sea.

Janey phoned tonight; she wanted to apologize for her short-time companion Tom who, she said, was in Oakland for a meeting last week and saw me in his hotel but didn't have time to come over and speak. He hoped I wasn't "peeved." (Ugly, inappropriate word—I may be displeased or angry, I'm surely never "peeved.") I told Janey that was quite all right, since it hadn't been me.

"You didn't see Tom in Oakland last week, Mom?"

"No. As a matter of fact, darling, I don't think I've ever been in Oakland."

"Really? Tom was positive it was you. He said you looked right at him and smiled."

"Someone may have looked right at him, but it wasn't me."

"I guess you must have a double, Mom," said Janey, laughing. "They say everyone does, somewhere in the world."

I didn't laugh. Instead I felt a sort of shiver; why? Something unpleasant about the idea that everyone has a double, if it's true—which I doubt in my case, though one does often meet people who seem to be cut from a standard Simplicity or Butterick pattern.

Or did the chill come from the realization that my lovely Janey is living with one of those muddleheaded mortals who can't see the world clearly? They literally can't tell an oak from an elm, or a goose from a swan, so any woman in her forties with thick flowing dark hair, wide-set hazel eyes, and a longish pale striking face might register as "Karo McKay/Janey's mother."

The idea of doubling. In poetry it can be beautifully satisfying: the refrain, the villanelle—most of all when on each reappearance the line has a subtly altered meaning. In life? Twins, mirror images—I would hate to be a twin, though Janey as a child once wished she were. It would be company, she said.

Body doubles in the films, for modest actresses or those whose bodies aren't ideal. Or stand-ins, sparing the performer boredom and annoyance before the cameras turn. That could be convenient— To have a stand-in who would take my place for all the tedious chores that go with giving a reading but aren't mentioned in the contract: someone who would be polite and charming to the nervous students who meet the flight, make conversation at long receptions, sign books, give interviews to local newspapers and radio stations— Yes, that's what I'd wish for, if wishes were horses— Pegasus?

OCTOBER

BACK FROM OHIO, a half-satisfactory trip. Reasonably intelligent and appreciative audience, unreasonable weather. Drenching thunderstorms, the entire campus vibrating and flashing and sloshing about like a sinking liner. I stepped from some thoughtless professor's car into half a foot of foul water, and had to come onstage trailing yards of sodden white lace and with my new satin slippers soaked and muddied.

Yet worse, they'd put me in an immense hall. I spoke to a hundred bodies and perhaps three times that many empty seats. Though I knew the storm had kept people away, I continuously had to repel the thought that my sponsors had expected Karo McKay to draw a larger crowd and were disappointed. In me. So much better when the auditorium is somewhat too small, standing room only, and everyone has the sense of being at an important event; how the energy builds then!

Not really glad to be back here. The weather's improved, but not my apartment, and I haven't finished a poem since August. Near-strangers keep asking (don't they know how impolite this is, how hurtful?), "What are you writing now?"

"Oh, I'm working on something," I lie.

Also, I'm discouraged by the local literary scene. The fiction people are overrun with small children, and haven't been especially forthcoming. There are also three poets in the department: but the best one's out of town and the others seem to look upon me mainly as a professional resource (recommendations, advice on grants and fellowships and writers' colonies). They aren't in the least interested in me, want to talk about their careers, their reviews, their students, their publications (slim limp small-press volumes).

Why did I come here, why didn't I stay in my enchanted cottage on the silver pond? Because I thought I couldn't afford to. I believed that if I wanted to exist above subsistence level I couldn't, daren't turn down a job. Not that I need much; I care nothing for the latest car or kitchen appliance. But if I'm to work well I must have a warm, quiet room flowing with soft music; the scent and color of fresh flowers; simple but perfect meals with good wine; the look and feel of almond silk and lace and taffeta against my skin.

But this is the last time. With the lecture fees Bryan Wood can—so easily, it seems!—arrange, I need never again be a Visiting Poet (that anomalous role, something like a Visiting Nurse, something like a Visiting Diplomat). I need never again live among repellent shapes and sounds and odors, among people whose voices and faces sandpaper my nerves.

One example: an unsettling incident today in the department office. As I was collecting my mail one of the secretaries came over and noisily thanked me for signing a copy of *Moon Thunder* for her mother.

"Your mother?—" I tried to search my memory bank, but I must have signed twenty or thirty books in Ohio.

"Maybe Moms didn't mention my being here; she was probably too excited. But she was really thrilled with what you wrote. She's a poet herself—well, you know that."

How did I know that, I wondered. "Oh? What did I write?"

"You said: 'With best wishes to a budding poetess.' "

"Really?" I frowned; was I losing my mind? "This was in Columbus, Ohio, last week?"

"No no, in Denver. Moms lives in Denver."

"There must be some mistake," I said pleasantly. "I didn't give a reading in Denver last week; I was in Ohio."

"Oh, it wasn't at a reading. It was in a bookstore. There's this very fine bookstore in Denver, you know, and Moms saw you there. She recognized you from your picture. Anyhow, I just wanted to thank you—"

"You're welcome, but—" I began. Then the girl's phone started ringing, and I departed to puzzle the thing out.

I thought at first that it was simply a mistake: "Moms" must have met a poet with a similar name (Carolyn Kizer? Carolyn Forche?). Then another possibility occurred to me: that some woman in Denver had been taken for me and decided to play along. I suppose it's the sort of thing a certain sort of person might do on impulse, to have the temporary sensation of being a well-known writer.

A dreadful idea. To be imitated like that—and what's worse, falsified—for whoever sees that phony inscription will think I, Karo McKay, used a vulgar cliché like "budding poetess." I detest the word "poetess" and "budding" is a wholly dead image—or if live, a hideous one: Daphne covered with acne lumps of half-formed leaf. And surely neither Carolyn F. nor Carolyn K. would write such a phrase.

Also, neither they nor I would ever write that some complete stranger was a poet, budding or otherwise. Noncommittal blandness, that's the only policy. Though there have been times when I've had the impulse to scribble something insulting. When someone's been really obnoxious, holding up the line, wanting to argue stupidly and lengthily—

Or even worse, when book dealers appear with six or eight first editions wrapped in clammy transparent plastic. Sometimes they don't even trouble to attend the reading, merely skulk about outside and then, when I appear, rush in ahead of everyone else. They heave their stack of volumes onto the table and push the title pages at me one after the other, always asking that I include the place and date as well as my name, which apparently increases their markup. "With worst wishes" or even "Your enemy" are phrases that have passed through my mind at these moments.

Meanwhile I suppose I must return to the department office and tell the secretary that her mother was deceived, my book defaced. Dismally embarrassing, painful for everyone. And is it even possible? Not only don't I know her name, I'm not absolutely sure which of the three young women there she is. They look rather alike really, and I was distressed at the time—

So I'll have to let the matter rest. And after all, who will see that phony inscription? At the most, only a few obscure souls somewhere in Colorado.

Then why do I feel harm has been done? I think because the ceremony of book-signing isn't just a formality. It sometimes seems that way: all my fans do is thank me for the reading and hold out a volume of poems (and usually a scratchy Bic, which is why I always bring my italic pen). They're far more innocent than the dealers, of course. They don't intend to sell the book; might even be shocked at the idea. For them it's a sort of ritual. The volume a poet has touched and signed develops an instant invisible aura, becomes a minor sort of holy icon in the religion of poetry.

A religion, yes, or at least a cult, with its own temples and altars, its dead saints, its living hierarchy of priests and priestesses; its deacons, vergers, and sextons (the critics), and its statistically small but devout congregations. Yes, and the rare-book dealers are like those shoddy sellers of religious goods whose shops you see near European cathedrals—not true believers, merely peddlers with a sharp eye to profits.

And I am a part of it all—a member of the Poetrian clergy: priestess, prophetess. Hence the sense of sacrilege I feel at the idea of some dishonest laywoman (or perhaps even an infidel) donning invisible false vestments, pretending to consecrate *Moon Thunder* with my name.

NOVEMBER

AWAY for three hectic days in the Midwest. Two successful readings, one less so. The trouble began at the pre-reading dinner, where there was a really irritating faculty wife: a self-satisfied, preening straw-blonde in a floor-dragging tawny mink coat that surely involved the murder of at least twenty innocent animals. Immensely pleased with herself and greedily garrulous; she actually interrupted me twice in mid-sentence.

I forgot her for most of the performance, but when I came to "The Leopard" I remembered and gave her an accusing sibyl's stare. She only smirked and nestled further into her soft silvery fur. Somehow that broke the spell; I went on effectively, but for the first time in years with conscious effort, as if I were acting a part, pretending to be Karo McKay. Only for a minute or two, but it was disagreeable, disorienting.

Perhaps it didn't always work for the sibyls either. Perhaps sometimes, confronting some shallow, self-satisfied person, they suddenly weren't inspired and possessed, but merely tired and strained, breathing with difficulty in the hot odorous smoke, projecting their voices, moving in the motions.

Otherwise all went well. Agreeable hosts, large loving audiences—yes, it is love I feel coming from them as I stand in the spotlight, in some ways as satisfying as any I've known. Compared to that generous anonymous outpouring, other loves appear flawed and greedy. The older I grow, the less romantic physical sex seems to me. It grabs, shoves itself at one like those rare-book dealers (three of them at the last reading). But, worse than them, it wants me to inscribe a name—theirs—on my body, my soul. Then it packs up and takes off.

I'm beginning to realize that for me sensuality has always meant more than sex, been a deeper experience, focusing not only, not even most often, on another person, but on whatever is physically subtle and fine: the perfumed ivory satin of a camellia, a sudden sweet penetration of flute or cello, the taste of a tangerine warmed in the sun, the furred touch of grass, the pure green light after rain, and the sharp, almost sour scent of wet oak leaves. That's how one should be, surely: open to the multitudinous sensual delights of the world.

A STRANGE and annoying bill came this afternoon, from a store in Minneapolis: "Sweater . . . $39.00." "I still remember our very good talk," said the note stapled to it. "Hope you haven't forgotten this." Well, I did remember accompanying that pleasant woman from the Arts Council into a shop after lunch, but surely I made no purchase. Was I losing my memory?

Or was there a more likely but equally unpleasant explanation: that the woman who impersonated me in Denver and wrote "budding poetess" in a copy of *Moon Thunder* was now in Minneapolis and pretending again to be Karo McKay? It could happen; one reads about things like that.

What might such a woman be like? Lonely, needy, obviously a misfit. No, not obviously, or she couldn't deceive anyone—though perhaps this doesn't apply, because ordinary people expect oddness in artists. Possibly she has fantasized being a famous writer.

Suppose she was intoxicated with the success of her first, impulsive masquerade in the bookshop in Denver. Then this month, in Minneapolis, she saw my poster in a shop window and tried the same act deliberately— Perhaps not so much in order to steal a sweater as to have the intoxicating experience of being Karo McKay again.

What was most dreadful was the idea that someone could pass herself off as me and get away with it. I couldn't think what to do, could barely swallow supper. Finally I phoned Janey. "That woman, you know, the one who pretended to be me in Denver, she's at it again," I said, trying but failing to speak in a calm, even amused tone.

Janey, being rational and unimaginative like her father (I often regret this inheritance, but I suppose it has advantages), treated my story as the joke I half-tried to make it, and suggested that my first explanation might have been correct.

"Maybe you just forgot, you know, Mom, like with the lime tree," she said, recalling that incident years ago when my father was so ill. I went into a flower store to find something to take to the hospital, and then was overcome by a beautiful fragrant living presence. But by the time I'd got home from seeing Dad it had gone totally out of my head.

The lime tree arrived that evening, causing Janey, then four, to announce to a roomful of relatives and guests, "Mommy, there's a man here with a big bush for you." It was an amusing family story, back when we were an amusing family. Later it became first an example of my hopeless absentmindedness, then one of the things my former husband threw up against me. Yes, threw, like a series of stale cream pies in some low farce.

"That might be possible," I told Janey. "Except I haven't got a new sweater."

"Maybe the store is waiting for your check," Janey suggested.

"Well, I'm not going to send one," I said. Because if I

write a check I lose either way. Either some garment I don't need will come, proving that my memory is failing; or it won't, proving that I have been impersonated and ripped off.

Hideous weather here now. Cold throbbing rain or half-snow, trees sifted down into sodden heaps, sky lowered like a water-stained canvas circus tent. And I'm stuck in the circus doing my ringmistress act, snapping my whip four times a week at rooms full of performing tigers— No, nothing so interesting: seals. Rewarding them with a bit of fishy praise when they blow some simple tune on their row of brass trumpets. Mainly though it's discords, poetic burps and farts—and the little seals all so proud of their cacophony!

Meanwhile I'm not blowing any tunes myself. (Distressed about this, don't think about this.)

DECEMBER

IT'S HAPPENED AGAIN. Today I received a holograph love letter from some man in Chicago called—hard to tell from the signature—Hal or Hull. No other name or return address, only the postmark. "My wonderful dearest," it began, "it's 3 A.M. but I can't sleep, thinking of you, the sheets still warm where you lay looking at me with your great topaz cat's eyes. How lucky I am, how fantastic you were . . ." It went on in this vein for over a page, moderately erudite (ending with a line from Byron), romantic, sensual, occasionally edging toward pornographic, and clearly addressed to some woman Hal or Hull had just been intimate with for the first time.

At first, reading this letter, I had a frightening fantasy. I think because of the topaz eyes. I imagined that it was really addressed to me, that I was suffering from pernicious amnesia and that somehow somewhere in the Middle West

I had spent a night with an unknown man. I almost persuaded myself that I remembered, that stormy night in Chicago when I was so exhausted and shaky, some large fellow with his arm round me, helping me out of a car into a moonglow whirl of snow— Beyond that, nothing.

I suppose I also imagined this because of occasional encounters in the past—that time in Toronto, the amazing Belgian—or the famous poet in Cambridge, long before I was famous— I don't often think of those moments now; they were impulsive detours, not on my real route. And nowadays I would surely never— For one thing, the chance of distasteful, even disastrous medical results.

Then I knew what had really happened. That psychotic kleptomaniac woman who impersonated me in the store in Minneapolis, and wrote "budding poetess" in somebody's copy of *Moon Thunder* in Denver, had been in Chicago. She'd been pretending to be Karo McKay again, and picked up some man who now believes he made love to me. No doubt it was easy to attract him that way: people adore the idea of being romantically involved with a poet—they imagine verses dedicated to them, their name preserved in anthologies.

Yes, and now Hal/Hull will boast about this pickup—her bold approach, his easy conquest, his hot night with "Karo McKay"—to everyone who will listen. The tale will go round, will be elaborated on, will spread. One day, Hal/Hull will be in my biography.

Janey was wrong: Not-Karo exists. She is out there somewhere in the Midwest, moving through the winter and the darkening light. Maybe in Denver her masquerade was only the casual impulse of a moment. But now she's planning it, enjoying it, getting more skilled, taking ever greater chances, without caring about the effect on my reputation. She deliberately walked off with that sweater, knowing that if I don't pay for it for the rest of my life some shopkeeper in Minnesota will despise (and describe) Karo McKay as a deadbeat.

Or perhaps it's not only opportunism, but actual malice. Not-Karo wants to make me look bad, get me in trouble. Perhaps she's Not-Fan as well. Perhaps she's someone else's fan, or she thinks I was rude to her somewhere, or she took something I wrote or said personally—people do that. If you become famous, you acquire unknown enemies as well as unknown friends.

Perhaps Not-Karo actually hates me, the way so many members of the public, sometimes without even knowing it, envy and hate writers and artists. Because our lives are more interesting and meaningful than theirs, because we're loved and rewarded for what to them looks like mere play. Doing what we like: not holding down a full-time job, not having to please the boss, getting away with things.

And now Not-Karo has experienced firsthand the public rewards of being a writer—strangers in bookshops approaching her with awe and admiration, shopkeepers trusting her with merchandise, interesting men becoming eager and desirous at first sight— She's not going to stop now, why should she? Next time she may use my name to buy something wildly expensive or sleep with someone coarse and vulgar, or do something even more indelicate and awful, so awful I can't even imagine it now.

No, she's not just some sad lost creature. She's deranged, of course, but not obviously so, and full of cunning and spite. Also she vaguely resembles me, and knows enough about my life and work to impersonate me successfully. And she's either financially independent or has a job that makes it possible—even necessary?—for her to travel from one Midwestern city to another. Denver—Minneapolis—Chicago.

What if Not-Karo is also the woman Janey's Tom saw in Oakland? Sitting in some hotel, deliberately got up as Karo

McKay— If that's so, she's not limited to the Midwest; she could appear anywhere, anytime. And what's so hopeless, so horrible, there's nothing I can do about it.

JANUARY

SANCTUARY at last on Cape Cod. The term's ended, two batches of performing seals disposed of (though two new ones will be waiting for me back at Convers College next week). Tranquil Christmas with Janey and her friend Tom, who seems to have become a household fixture (clothes hook? door latch?). Pale fine winter, the sky and pond and clouds shimmering, subtle shades of silver, ice-green, azure.

The day after Janey arrived I told her about Not-Karo's latest exploit. I'd been dreading that she would suggest I was losing my memory again, but she had a much simpler explanation: the billet-doux had got into the wrong envelope, as I'm afraid my checks (but never hers, of course) sometimes do.

If she's right, My Wonderful Dearest has received a polite business letter from Hal/Hull—inviting me to read at his college, for instance. This harmless missive presumably has my name and address typed out, so Dearest will know what's happened. She'll be embarrassed, angry at Hal/Hull. And disappointed: a man who makes that kind of error after one night's acquaintance isn't a good risk for a long-term relationship, one would imagine. Janey also suggested that probably Dearest, if she has any sense of responsibility, will forward my real letter.

"And I suppose you don't believe in the woman in Oakland either," I said.

"Absolutely not," declared Janey, and she pointed out that whoever smiled at Tom in the hotel couldn't possibly have known of his connection with me. Moreover now Tom had changed his story. "She didn't look all that much like you anyhow," he told me. "She was heavier, for one thing."

"I've lost weight this fall," I said; but I felt soothed, relieved. "Very well, darling. If you look at it your way there's a rational explanation for each incident. But what troubles me is that there are so many of them, and they seem to make a pattern."

"I know what you mean," agreed Janey. "But really, Mom, I think it's just coincidence."

Suppose that's so. Things that really don't match, superimposed to make a false design. And as Janey also pointed out before she left, nothing that might fit such a design has happened for well over a month.

"You've been working too hard and traveling too much, I think," Janey said; and she's right. I must pace myself, cut out all those extraneous unpaid activities that have nothing to do with my real work in life, which is to write and read poetry. Politely decline to give lectures, be on panels, sign petitions, fill in questionnaires, judge student writing contests, donate books or manuscripts to be auctioned for some worthy cause, or contribute a poem to some pale new magazine.

For a start, I must write to say that I can't possibly speak at the county library benefit or judge the high school Poetry Award. And ask Bryan Wood to cancel my expenses-only talk to the Volunteers for Literacy in Detroit next month. He'll be cross, because it's all arranged: the flights, the hotel— Perhaps it would be better to wait until the last minute, tell him I'm ill; everyone's sympathetic when you're ill.

I'm alone here now and at peace, watching the cloud shadows skate on the pond. The gulls wheeling and dipping above, living grey and white origami kites. What still troubles me though, comes between me and the page when I sit at my desk, are recurring images of Not-Karo. Even if she doesn't exist, never existed, she exists in my mind, a grey flapping kite, blocking out the few words I've scratched on the white page. And if I'm not writing, I'm as unreal, or as much of an impostor, as she is.

FEBRUARY

THE DEAD DARK of winter. Yet another storm outside the apartment complex. Whirling flakes, clots of snow sliding down the black glass as if some monster were spitting on my window.

Also a bad, frightening thing has happened. Yesterday my old college friend Merry Carson sent me a clipping from the Detroit paper, with a terse note complaining that after all these years of declining to visit her I'd been in town without letting her know, speaking at a lunch to promote literacy.

Except of course I wasn't there. Two days before the event I called Bryan to wail that I had the flu and couldn't make it. I even, at his suggestion, phoned the woman in Detroit to say I was desolated and pledge my support.

Truly, I wasn't there. But here was the apparent proof: a women's-page article with an unflattering picture of me and a horrible, unrecognizable quote, nothing like what I'd said on the phone.

> 'The other speakers have emphasized the practical advantages of literacy,' declared Miss [not "Ms.," not even Mrs.] McKay, 'but in my personal opinion, what's most meaningful about literacy is that it puts you in real human contact with the world of literature. For example, once you know how to read you can, hopefully, forge a personal relationship with great contemporary American poets like Adrienne Rich and Denise Levertov.'

Besides everything else that's truly awful about this state-ment—jargon, repetition, defunct metaphor—there's the assertion that Adrienne and Denise are great American poets. *Good,* I could have said, or even *important.* Never *great,* that's for the future to judge.

I called Merry at once and told her the truth, that I'd known for a month that I couldn't manage Detroit but had waited until the last minute to cancel so as not to infuriate Bryan. I suggested that the newspaper had confused the story, attributed someone else's remarks to me. But Merry wasn't soothed, wasn't convinced. I could hear her think-ing: Lying to her agent, lying to me. She agreed that the quote didn't sound much like me ("but then, Carrie, I haven't seen you in nearly ten years, have I?"—aggrieved tone here).

Besides, Merry thought the ideas in the quote were ex-actly like mine. "You know how you were always claiming that art was more important than security and family hap-piness," she announced, reminding me that even in college she used to maintain the opposite view. I thought then it was just for the sake of argument—but now she has five children and a Tudor castle in Grosse Pointe. And when I think how we used to be Carrie Martin and Merry Carson in Bertram Hall, almost twin-named freshman roommates, soulmates, inseparable!

Next I phoned the Detroit newspaper. The woman I eventually reached was polite at first but unhelpful. She hadn't written that story, hadn't been to the luncheon, didn't know who had. Oh no (less polite), they were always careful to check their facts. No, she couldn't promise that they'd print a retraction—she'd have to consult her boss. What did I say my name was? (huffy, suspicious). At this I became so upset that I raised my voice—actually, I more or less started to scream. Which of course made her sure I was an impostor.

An impostor. All right. Suppose it wasn't just an editorial mix-up. Suppose it was Not-Karo again, suppose she does exist and is still impersonating me all over the country and making me look terrible. Only now she's not content with making me look terrible to one person at a time. She wants to reach a wider audience. The public self has a life of its own, I remember someone saying that. And now Not-Karo is becoming my public self, in order to destroy me.

Near panic, I phoned Bryan Wood and told him nearly the whole story. At first he was very irritating, suggesting that sick and feverish as I had been (I couldn't tell him the truth about this of course), I'd really given that turgid statement. When I denied this, he grudgingly considered the possibility of an impostor, but hadn't any suggestion for dealing with the situation, and (under his professionally solicitous condolences) seemed actually to find it amusing. "It's the price of fame, I suppose," he said, and gave a snuffly giggle, covering it with a cough and the remark (lie? both of us lying about being ill?) that he had a bad cold. When I asked if he thought I should go to the police he said he didn't see much future in that.

"Now let's get this clear," he said (I could hear him trying not to laugh). "You're proposing to complain to the Detroit cops that some woman may have posed as you and told a reporter that Denise and Adrienne" (also his clients, incidentally) "are great poets? Confidentially, Karo, I don't quite see it." (Another giggle, or sneeze.) "I think if I were you I'd try to forget the whole thing. Even if this person exists, she really hasn't done you much damage."

"No, she only made me look like an utter fool and a terrible writer, and stole a sweater in Minneapolis and told some woman in Denver that she was a budding poetess," I said; I was unable to mention the letter from Hal/Hull.

"I thought you'd decided that was a case of mistaken identity."

"I did at first, but— Oh, never mind." I gave up; hung up, took another V. (Must refill my prescription again.) As soon as Janey should have been home from work, I phoned her, but couldn't get through until after eleven. And then she wasn't any help.

"I think it was probably just a mistake, Mom," she said. "The publicity people assumed you'd be there, so they turned in a press release early. They do that in my office sometimes. SIXTY LOBBY FOR ABORTION RIGHTS, somebody sent that out last month, and then there was a blizzard and half of us couldn't get to the statehouse. But it was printed in the *Globe* and they didn't correct it."

Besides, it had to be a mistake, Janey said, because even if Not-Karo existed, and was in Detroit, and knew that you were going to speak there, why would she have wanted to give the newspaper a false statement?

"Because she hates me, because she wants to make me look bad," I said.

There was a silence on the phone, but I could hear what Janey was thinking; I remembered her four-year-old voice saying for the first, but not the last time, "Mommy's silly." And then I heard her twenty-six-year-old voice saying that I mustn't worry, that I must try to put it out of my mind and get some sleep. Which was what she probably wanted herself, so I said I would and good night.

Off balance; mocked or suspected by everyone, that's how I feel. Unsure of myself, of the truth. Which I suppose is what Not-Karo wants me to feel. And the clues keep coming in. For instance, I've never received the respectable letter from Hal/Hull that Janey predicted.

About midnight, unable to sleep, I found an old road map of the United States in a drawer. Oakland—Denver—Minneapolis—Chicago—Detroit. Finally I saw the pattern: I saw that Not-Karo was moving eastward, moving toward me. Coming to get me, for some crazy reason, for the reason that she's crazy.

MARCH

CHILL DRENCHING RAINS, low and confused in spirit. I've had a viscid cold for weeks. Still intermittently feverish, barely meeting my classes. Not-Karo hasn't manifested herself again in any way I can tell anyone of, yet what happened last week in Buffalo has left a fog of fear over my life, especially whenever I appear in public.

It was in the Buffalo airport. As I entered the terminal I saw, fifty feet away behind the barrier, two obvious young academic types, one carrying a white placard—evidently my welcoming committee. Then I saw them approach and greet someone else, a dark-haired woman only visible to me from behind, who after a moment walked on, leaving them to stare about and then wave tentatively at me. A minor case of mistaken identity, they explained as I stood there, nearly unable to speak.

Because a shudder of dread had gone through me: Not-Karo. I was only safe, I thought, because I hadn't seen her face; if I'd seen her face I would have died.

Don't be silly, it couldn't have been Not-Karo, I told myself on the way to town. She might have known I was giving a reading in Buffalo; she couldn't have known what plane I was arriving on. But whoever that woman was, if she had claimed to be Karo McKay they would have accepted her and left me standing in the terminal as if I didn't exist.

At the motel I still felt strained, strange. Took a little V, lay down on the bed but couldn't relax, got up, put on my cream lace dress and French chandelier earrings, brushed out my hair, redid my makeup, sprayed myself with Ma Griffe. In the glass I looked like Karo McKay.

But all through what followed I didn't feel like her. The food at the official dinner tasted strange, and whenever I spoke to anyone I felt as if I was reading from a script, a script I'd read from too often before.

Then when I came onstage it was wrong from the start. I could see the hands clapping in the half-dark, but they sounded like canned TV applause. There was no transforming rush and glow of energy, nothing. I smiled, spoke, started the tape. But as I gestured, as I modulated and projected my voice, every word sounded false, every movement was like time-lapse photography, artificially slowed down or speeded up.

And then, toward the end of the reading, I had this sensation that it wasn't me the audience was staring at, it was someone else, someone standing just behind me and a little to the left. I felt frightened, dizzy, literally dragged myself through the final two poems. As I left the stage I glanced over my shoulder; no one was there. But everything was still wrong; all the praises and thanks afterward, and my replies, seemed coerced and artificial. I can't do this anymore, I thought; I can't go on.

But I must go on. The world demands that I exhibit myself regularly onstage, and at the obligatory accompanying parties, lunches, dinners, receptions. It threatens me with poverty and obscurity if I don't perform, and bribes me with fame and fees—sometimes more for one reading than most of my books earn in years.

And it's not only me. Haven't I seen how many good writers—great writers—have gone on appearing in public far more often and longer than they should, because of these bribes and threats? Haven't I seen them onstage, worn down, slowed down physically and emotionally, stumbling and repeating themselves? Exhausting themselves, so that they haven't the energy or tranquillity to write? It could happen to me. Maybe it's already begun to happen, and that's why I can't— Don't think about it.

Everything I felt in Buffalo can be explained rationally, no doubt: that I was tired, airsick, getting over a cold, had too much to drink, etc. But what I can't explain is the absolute terror of that moment at the airport when I thought I saw the back of Not-Karo, whoever she was. Or what. She resembled a normal woman, but suppose she wasn't.

Suppose she never was real, but was, is, a kind of vampire or specter, moving toward me. Oakland—Denver—Minneapolis—Chicago—Detroit . . . Buffalo. And in an almost straight line. Not a human being at all, but an evil spirit, like those demons in oriental folklore who can't turn corners.

That would explain how she always knows where I am, how she can slide from city to city. Spreading slime wherever she goes like a crawling snail, souring and destroying my life. So that once she's done the public things, I become unable to do them; it's as if they've been slimed and fouled. Already I can't smile at attractive strangers, sign books, or speak to fans in the easy, graceful way I once did. And now even being onstage feels false.

No, no, I mustn't think that way, that's mad. I've been ill, I must give myself time to recover. Call Bryan, cancel those last two readings. Yes, and tell him to hold off for a while on scheduling anything for the summer or fall. Panic: if I can't perform, can't teach, how will I survive?

And I daren't take too much time off. If I don't appear anywhere, gradually I'll cease to exist as far as the literary world is concerned. Lovers of poetry are as restless and fickle as most lovers; if you don't continually remind them of your existence they soon forget you. Especially if you haven't written any new— (Don't think about that.) Sooner than you can imagine you're unknown.

APRIL

IT'S OVER, everything's over, my writing my life everything. I made a fatal error: I let Bryan Wood persuade me not to cancel the Albany reading. He was so shocked, so insistent, telling me over and over that it was so near, so important, so well paid.

"I'm thinking of you, Karo darling," he said, "your reputation," but wasn't he really thinking of his own reputation for being able to produce performing poets reliably?

Even on the plane I suspected I'd made a terrible mistake. We began to lurch through cold boiling clouds and I opened the airsick magazine to the map scored with spidery routes and traced that particular strand of the web. Oakland—Denver—Minneapolis—Chicago—Detroit—Buffalo . . . Albany. Again I was moving toward Not-Karo, who was moving toward me.

And in Albany, from the first moment, everything was wrong, the air soupy white with spring fog like spoilt vichyssoise, people's faces and voices foggy. I was still queasy, and when I put on my sea-green silk in the motel room it hung round me like some sea nymph's discarded washing—I was still losing weight—and my face in the mirror was bruised and painted. I'm not well, I thought, I shouldn't have come.

Lay down, got up, swallowed another little V, no visible effect. Unlocked the miniature fridge, found a miniature bottle of orange juice and one of vodka, poured them together, became minimally able to function. Then the reception and dinner, with more drinking and talking and canned laughing. I heard myself talking and laughing too, but as if someone else, some ventriloquist, were doing it at a distance while I tried to sit upright and not be sick in my plate.

At the building where I was to read I asked for a washroom. Someone pointed the way, down a bare ill-lit corridor, a long hot stuffy space, rows of beige tiles, beige sinks, beige metal doors, all of them closed as if people with no feet were sitting inside the cubicles. I felt hot, dizzy, nauseous. Tried to vomit, couldn't, turned on the water and splashed myself. It didn't change anything, except that now my reflection in the long mirror was splashed and distorted, with stringy wet hair, the eyes yellow, unfocused.

I can't do it, I thought. I staggered into the corridor, ran in the other direction, turning, a dead end, turned again, into a cavernous curved space. Crowds crowding in. I slid and crowded through them, toward an open door.

Outside it was mercifully cooler. The fog was shredding, lifting, everything damp, dark, shining spring-flecked trees. I stood, swallowing cold clear air. For God's sake, Karo McKay, I thought, what the hell are you doing? You go back in there and read your poems like you promised.

So I stumbled back up the rain-speckled sidewalk. The lobby was almost empty now, and I started through the doors opposite, but a bulky young man on the other side blocked my way, demanded my ticket.

"Oh, I don't need a ticket, I'm the poet." I smiled. He didn't smile, or move.

"Sorry, ma'am. No free admission tonight. The box office is right over there. Better hurry, it's about to start."

I thought, Very well, I'll buy a ticket, they'll pay me back, it'll be a joke— But I had no money with me, only my brocade folder of poems and tape recorder. "You don't understand," I said, dizzy and nauseous again. "I'm the poet who's reading here—I'm Karo McKay."

The usher glanced at the poster on the wall, comparing the photo (years younger, pounds heavier) with me; it was clear that in his opinion they didn't remotely mesh. "Sorry, ma'am," he repeated in the flat voice one uses for gate-crashers and crazies.

He might have said more, but a gaggle of people was now hastening across the lobby with tickets extended. As he held the door wide for them I heard a woman's voice inside speaking, no, I thought, reading the first verse of "Distant Pleasures." That's my voice, I thought, from the tape I made for the Poetry Library, they're playing it to keep the audience quiet till I come.

I squeezed past the ticket-taker, pretending not to hear his protests, and stumbled down the aisle. But when I looked up at the stage a woman was already standing there, also with a bush of dark hair, a green dress, moving her arms around— I screamed, slipped, grabbed the wooden curve of a seatback, fell. Other people screamed, crowded round— It was over.

EXHAUSTION, the flu, everyone said afterward politely, sympathetically. I suppose behind my back some of them also said drugs, drink, breakdown, who knows? I don't remember the rest of it very well. At some point I was throwing up into a metal wastebasket, in a sort of seminar room with words in a foreign language chalked on the board. Or perhaps I'd just forgotten how to read, because I couldn't understand most of what people were saying to me either.

Later there was the backseat of a car with gum wrappers on the floor, and then a dowdy little bedroom with pink venetian blinds drawn and a pink candlewick bedspread, cups of lukewarm tea I pushed away.

But I couldn't sleep. I was sweating, running a fever, kept seeing Not-Karo, hearing her voice over and over and over. Horrible, and not just the voice, but the words, my words. It was as if I was hearing "Distant Pleasures" deliberately read wrong, in a false, theatrical manner, so that it sounded phony, inflated, second-rate.

I lay there in the dark, too hot and sick to sleep, hearing other lines of mine in my head, echoing and repeating as if in some infernal auditorium. They sounded out flawed and false, like the false name "Karo McKay," part stolen (from Janey's father) and never returned, part invented. And it seemed to me that every line I'd ever written or read was flawed and false: a pastiche of sentimental and melodramatic words soaked in overdramatic style like Karo syrup, cheap and sweet and sticky and colorless.

For a long time I lay there, sunk into the bed, and the light changed from night to day, and Janey came from Boston. She spoke with the doctor, she arranged everything. She also insisted that the woman in the green dress was only the professor who was supposed to introduce Karo McKay; that her dress wasn't green anyhow, but blue, and her hair was lighter than mine and only shoulder length. I'm not so sure. I think I saw what I saw. What I was supposed to see.

THEN JANEY CAME BACK to the apartment complex with me; later she helped me pack, and she and Tom drove me to Cape Cod. They or somebody must have sorted everything out, got the cottage opened and the heat turned on; somebody must have taught my last two weeks of classes.

I suppose Bryan Wood apologized to the Albany people. I don't know; I haven't wanted to speak to him, and he probably doesn't want to speak to me. I don't care. I prefer to think how I'll never again have to make lively conversation with deadly stupid strangers, jolt up and down on dwarf planes, and lie awake on rock-hard giant beds in airless anonymous motel rooms, listening to the asthmatic rattle of the air conditioner and trucks choking and wheezing out on some dirty unknown highway.

IT'S TRUE SPRING HERE. The pond shimmers with life, is shrill with birds, boisterous every evening with croaking frogs. I walk beside it, or in the thin wet woods among sawdust-covered unfurling spirals of bracken and red-veined skunk cabbage, dangerous with growth. I'm gaining weight, sleeping through the night again.

Haven't heard anything more of Not-Karo. Perhaps in destroying Karo McKay she's also been destroyed, dissolved "into thin air." No doubt Shakespeare was right: the air that phantoms dissolve into has to be especially thin, or they'd clog it like industrial pollutants.

At other times I think she was only a human impostor after all, and is still out there, lying to people, going on with Karo McKay's public life. I expect to come across her picture in the *Times,* read an interview, hear that someone's met her somewhere or been to a reading. I don't expect her to publish anything: impostors and evil spirits can't write poetry. And of course, if she doesn't publish, after a while everyone will forget her, even assume she is dead.

But it doesn't matter, because as far as I'm concerned she's already won. There's nobody here but Carrie Martin, a forty-eight-year-old divorced woman with a sensible and wonderful grown daughter. She knows shorthand and bookkeeping but is currently unemployed. She has a small —an inadequate—income, so she will have to look for some sort of work soon. She has pale dry skin and a long mop of dyed black hair growing out moss-grey, and used to be quite attractive. She wears reading glasses and has a partial plate. She doesn't accept mail addressed to Karo McKay. She likes orange-scented soap and white flowers and ripe avocados with lemon juice and olive oil. She has a vacant look in her eyes.

Her only problem is that lately she's started to hear phrases, lines, even whole stanzas of poetry, whispering at her everywhere—from the heaps of dusty potatoes and papery pale-auburn onions in the grocery, through the wet bluish mist over the pond. They won't let her alone; they echo, repeat themselves, shaping and reshaping themselves.

Usually she tries not to listen. But once in a while, to silence them, she scribbles them down and shuts them in a drawer. They want to get out, but she won't let them. Because as long as they're safe in the drawer, so am I.

Alison Lurie was born in 1926 in Chicago but grew up outside New York City. She was graduated from Radcliffe College in 1947 and subsequently worked as a librarian, editorial assistant, and secretary, and was associated with the Poets' Theatre of Cambridge. She then lived in a small college town in New England and in Los Angeles before settling in Ithaca, New York, where since 1970 she has taught literature, folklore, and writing at Cornell University. She is the author of eight novels: *Love and Friendship, The Nowhere City, Imaginary Friends, Real People, The War Between the Tates, Only Children, Foreign Affairs* (which won the Pulitzer Prize for Fiction), and *The Truth About Lorin Jones.* She is also the author of three collections of traditional folktales for children and two nonfiction books (*The Language of Clothes,* on the psychology of fashion, and *Don't Tell the Grown-Ups,* on children's literature), and her articles, stories, and reviews have appeared in many publications. The recipient of various awards and fellowships, she became a member of the American Academy of Arts and Letters in 1989.